Sarah Miller, Mail Order Bride

Vanessa Sarlson

Published by Trellis Publishing, 2021.

SARAH MILLER, MAIL ORDER BRIDE

First edition. July 10, 2021.

Copyright © 2021 Vanessa Sarlson.

ISBN: 979-8224394579

Written by Vanessa Sarlson.

Sarah Miller, Mail Order Bride

Vanessa Sarlson

SARAH MILLER, MAIL ORDER BRIDE

Chapter 1

Sarah could barely feel her fingers. They were blackened from work as each hour she stuffed teabag after teabag with a blend of bergamot. Around her were familiar faces. Most of the girls who worked at the factory happened to be orphans – abandoned at an early age.

The shift bell blared, indicating the end of the day. Sarah was the first one to gather up her things. She was out the door before the foreman could open it. With her head bent low, she filtered through the crowd of industrial workers. Most were headed home but she had a very different destination in mind.

The church tower chimed, announcing the hour.

Sarah quickened her pace.

She turned the corner and entered the main square. In her haste, she nearly got herself run over by a speeding carriage. The driver cursed in her direction but she shrugged off the insults and continued forward, a little more cautious this time.

In the distance, she spotted the postmaster general starting to close up shop for the day.

"Wait!" she called out.

He looked up and raised an eyebrow in question. "Lass, I'm closed."

"Please," she panted, winded from the sprint down the street. It became difficult for her to breathe as her throat seemed to tighten to the size of a spring twig. To keep from fainting, she bent over and placed her hands on her knees as she forced herself to inhale at a steady rhythm.

"Are you alright?" the man asked.

She straightened out, looking a bit pale. "Fine," she answered. "But I must pick up my mail," she said as she reached into her coin pouch. "Here."

He shook his head. "This is too much."

"Consider it payment for your troubles."

He insisted on returning the excess money. Sarah was about to say something in protest but he had already disappeared into the building.

"What's with all the hullabaloo?" he asked. "I've never seen anyone this adamant on getting their mail. There must be something important waiting for you."

"I certainly hope so." She held her breath as he sorted through the various letters.

"Sarah Miller, isn't it?"

"Yes," she said with a nod.

"I don't see anything..." He furrowed his brows together.

"Oh, but there must be – I am sure of it." She clung to the counter and rose to the tip of her toes. "Please..." she whispered more like a prayer than a plea.

"Unless it got sorted elsewhere. Just give me a moment," he excused himself and disappeared into the back room. She watched him moving from one place to another and it was making her horribly nervous.

She reached for the rosary that she always wore around her neck and started to finger the beads, silently whispering a prayer over each one.

"Ah, here it is," he said at last as he held out an envelope.

Sarah reached for it, her fingers trembling.

"Go on, it's not going to bite you."

Biting her bottom lip, she took it.

"Here." He offered her a letter opener.

Carefully, she pried open the seal and removed the letter she had been waiting for. The parchment paper was thick like it had been soaked by water during its travel to Liverpool. It crackled underneath her fingertips as she read through that familiar handwriting.

Dear Sarah,

I am writing this letter to inform you that you have been chosen as my wife. I await your arrival in Maine. We will marry as soon as you port and then we will travel to California where we will make a life for ourselves. It will not be easy but I have faith that you will be adept to handle whatever hardships that may come our way.

If you agree, send back a response. If you decide against our union, also send back a response.

Sincerely,

Aaron Mansfield

"Good news?" asked the postmaster.

"Very." Her eyes became glassy with tears. She wanted to hold them back but they ran down her cheeks, smudging the ink of Aaron's letter. She tried to wipe them away but it only made things worse. Half the letter was now unreadable.

"Here."

Sarah took the handkerchief and dabbed at her eyes. "Thank you."

"So, what's the good news."

"I am to travel to America to marry."

"Is that so?" he mused. "I hear it's a dangerous place. You be careful now, you hear?"

She nodded. "My husband will protect me."

"And do you know this bloke?"

"Not personally, no. In truth, he is a stranger." But Sarah did not care about that. She felt weightless with happiness. Finally, she was to belong to someone. Finally, she had a place where she belonged.

"Be careful," he repeated. "For this is a mighty big risk you're taking."

She nodded. "I will. I promise I will." She eyed the pen. "Mind if I write back a response?" She was already reaching into her coin pouch but the postmaster stopped her before she could pay him. "Sir?"

"Go ahead," he said as he prepared an envelope with postage. "It's on me."

"I cannot accept that," she countered. "We all work hard for our money and you are no exception."

He offered a smile. "I have spent my entire life a bachelor and I regret it more than anything else. I yearn for a wife to call my own but it's too late for that now. I've gone past my prime –"

"There's always time," she interrupted. "I'm sure you could find someone."

He shook his head. "Do not bother. Focus instead on your future and remember me when you say your vows. Do what I never did and enjoy every moment of it."

"I will," she promised before she lowered her head and began to pen her response. It took a bit of time but finally, she was happy with what she had written. "Wish me luck."

"You won't need it."

Chapter 2

Sarah's stomach churned as the waves crashed against the side of the ship. Like so many others, she wretched over the side of the railing and into the sea. Hungry fish nibbled at the mess before disappearing from sight.

When will it be over? she thought to herself.

Her legs wobbled as she struggled to make it below deck. There, the stench was horrible. She held a hand over her nose, trying to keep the smell from penetrating her nostrils. Still, they flared, angered by the pungency.

By some miracle, she managed to reach her room without spilling her guts all over the floor. Her head pounded as she laid down and stared at the bunk above hers. "Clarise?" she whispered but there was no response from her roommate. "Are you awake?"

A groan echoed through the room. Slowly, Sarah rose to her feet. Despite her best efforts, dizziness swept over her, blurring her surroundings. She steadied herself against the bed and blinked away the wave of nausea.

"Clarise," she said again, this time while resting her hand on the woman's forehead. "You're burning up!" she exclaimed as she pulled away her hand.

Sickness was running rampant through the ship. Already, halfway through the journey, countless had perished. Sarah was terrified that her newfound friend would be one of them.

"I..." Clarise tried to speak but her lips were so dry that they failed to move.

"Shh." Sarah placed a wet washcloth on her forehead. "Just rest for me, luv. That's all I want you to do," she whispered in a soothing voice as the young woman drifted into a fitful slumber.

***

Clarise never made it to the New World. Sarah carried a letter to her fiancé in her pocket. It pained her to deliver such news but she needed to tell the bloke that he was due to find himself a new wife. She did not even want to imagine the heartbreak this would cause him.

As they thoughts haunted her mind, she picked her suitcase and started down the ramp that connected to the dock. She swayed dangerously to the left, nearly falling right off the side. Luckily, there was someone there to catch her. His arms were strong and full of warmth. As he pulled her into his chest, she felt the thump of his heartbeat like the pounding of a drum.

"Are you alright, miss?" he asked.

She looked up and saw eyes as bright as the midmorning sky. Her cheeks colored as she found herself gravitating towards his face as a magnet pulled forward by the opposite pole.

He cleared his throat and stepped back.

"I'm sorry." Sarah's color deepened. "And thank you."

The man nodded. "Do you happen to know a Sarah Miller?"

"Yes," she said as she pointed to herself. "I am she."

He stepped back even further and this time, he looked her over like a butcher looking over a cut of meat.

Sarah didn't know what to do with herself then. His stare seemed to penetrate into her very soul. "Excuse me..." she whispered. "But I need to find my husband-to-be."

"You're looking at him," said Aaron. He couldn't help but smile at her thick accent.

Her eyes widened. "Oh!"

"Come, the chapel awaits."

She dug her feet into the ground. "Can it not wait a day? I have a letter I need to deliver."

"A letter?" he repeated as he raised his eyebrow in question. "To whom?"

"My roommate traveled across the Atlantic as I did – to get married – but she did not survive the trip."

Aaron's mood instantly darkened. He closed his eyes for a moment and pictured his late wife's smiling face. She had once been the sunshine of his life but now she was gone, only to be reunited in Heaven above. He clenched his fists to challenge the pain.

"I wrote him a letter and I would like to deliver it," she said. "He has the right to know what happened."

"Very well," Aaron conceded. "We will deliver it and then we will marry."

There was a certain coldness in his tone that made Sarah flinch. He did not seem pleased with her. Was it the way she looked? Or perhaps the way she dressed? Suddenly self-conscious, she followed her groom as they searched the crowd until they found the fellow who was still waiting for his wife-to-be to await from the ship.

"Mr. Lowell?"

"Yes?" He regarded the woman with interest but then saw she was already with another.

"I traveled with Clarise –"

"Do you know where she is?"

"She..." Sarah choked on her words as her chest tightened.

"She's dead," Aaron interjected in a calloused manner.

"No..." he whispered. "It cannot be..." his voice was hollow as he spoke. "We were childhood lovers. We had promised we would be together..." He pulled at his own hair. "And I insisted we come to America to start a better life and look where that got us."

"Sir..." Sarah reached forward to touch his arm but he snapped away.

"Leave me alone," he hissed before storming off.

"I was only trying to help."

"There is no greater pain than that of a man who has lost his wife," Aaron said in a somber tone. "It is a burning that cuts deep and stays with him into his final breath."

Sarah studied her husband-to-be. It sounded like he spoke from experience. She realized then that she knew very little about this man. She had been so eager to find someone to fill the emptiness of her life that she had not stopped to consider the repercussions of marrying a stranger.

Who was this man?

And could she learn to love him?

Chapter 3

A few hours later.

Sarah had not fully recovered from her trip and yet, she was already trussed up inside a wedding dress. It didn't quite fit the way it was supposed to and the hem was discolored like someone had worn it before.

"You look lovely," said one of the parishioners who had volunteered to help.

"Do I?" Sarah fused with her hair. Despite the few flowers she held in her hand, they felt extremely heavy.

"Certainly, dear." She smiled. "It'll be a happy marriage, I am sure of it."

And yet, as Sarah made her way towards the altar, Aaron did not look pleased to see her. There was a bitter sort of expression on his face. Not once did he smile in her direction. He kept his eyes trained on the priest and concentrated on keeping his thoughts tied to the present but they kept reminding him of the late wife he was leaving behind.

Was this a mistake?

What would she think if she knew he was moving on without her?

But he couldn't stand to live in that town of theirs any longer. Walking along those streets without her was driving him towards an early grave. It was time for him to start fresh somewhere else.

"I now pronounce you husband and wife." Aaron had drowned out most of the ceremony. Now, it was time for him to kiss his wife. His lips burned with betrayal. This woman was *not* Abigail. *What am I doing?* he thought to himself. But, nevertheless, with the entire church watching, he felt the obligation weigh heavily on his shoulders so he leaned forward and planted a fleeting kiss on her lips.

Sarah's heart soared for it was the first time she had ever experienced such intimacies. Her lips tingled and she yearned for more but Aaron had already gripped her hand. He towed her towards the exit where they were showered with a sprinkling of rice.

Aaron plowed through it and reached his horse within a moment's notice. Taking his wife by the hips, he hoisted her onto the saddle. A second later, he settled in behind her, arms tight around her body.

"Oh!" she exclaimed as her heart skipped a beat. She could feel every single inch of his body against hers. With burning cheeks, she tried not to dwell on the fact.

Without a word, Aaron dug his spurs into the horse's side and off they went. He rode through town. As a native of the little Maine town, he knew the way like the back of his hand. Everything about it was familiar.

With it came memories that he would rather forget.

Soon, they arrived at a cozy little cottage. "Here we are," he announced. He got down and helped Sarah to the ground.

Accidentally, her foot hitched against the ground and she fell forward, colliding into his chest.

He caught her by the arms and fell back a few steps. His balance was compromised and he crashed into the earth, Sarah still tightly encased in his arms.

Their faces were but inches apart. She could feel his warm breath against her lips, like an invitation calling her forward. She took up that invitation and closed the distance between them.

The kiss lasted but a moment before he pulled away, head shaking. "No," was all that he said as he got up and turned his back towards her. "There is one thing you should know before we move forward. I did not marry for love. I have given away my heart and there's nothing left for anyone else. So, our marriage is simply one of convenience. You are my ticket to California."

Sarah felt floored by his words. He had not disclosed any of this information during their correspondence. "But..."

"There will be no further discussion on the matter," he said. "We both need our rest for tomorrow we start our journey for the west." He took up her luggage bag and carried it into the guest room.

"Will we not even share a bed as a married couple?" she asked.

"No." He closed the door behind him. It rattled the doorframe.

Sarah's legs gave out as she collapsed onto the edge of her bed. She hung her head in her hands as tears ran down her cheeks. *Oh, how naïve I have been,* she thought to herself. *To think that someone could actually love me...*

***

The following morning.

Sarah awoke before the sun could crest over the horizon. She stood and watched as a golden wave of color washed over the land. It was so beautiful – more beautiful than she ever thought America could be. And yet, her dream was quickly turning into a nightmare. All her wishing for love and a place for her to belong was being shattered by her husband's coldness.

She pulled her shawl tight around her shoulders before finally leaving the room. She tiptoed towards the living room and stoked the fire back to life. With its light, she was able to see a portrait pinned above the mantel. She recognized Aaron but not the woman that stood beside him. There was a ring on her finger.

Ah, his wife, she realized. *The one he lost, perhaps.*

She wanted to learn their story but she did not feel comfortable broaching the topic with her husband. It seemed like a wound that had festered and it was better to keep from agitating it.

So, she walked away and entered the kitchen area. Soon, the smell of cooking thickened the area. She hummed to herself, forgetting the situation she now found herself in. Cooking always had a way of calming her nerves.

Aaron appeared by the kitchen table. Seeing Sarah move reminded him on Abigail and yet, there was something different about this woman. She had a sort of happiness that seemed to radiate from her very body.

He watched her and the hardness of his heart seemed to soften. Perhaps he deserved a second chance.

No, he told himself. *I vowed myself to Abigail and none other shall take her place.*

Chapter 4

That afternoon, they were all packed up and ready to go. Aaron loaded everything onto the back of a wagon whilst Sarah handed them over to him. "Why are you leaving such a cozy little home –"

He stopped her by raising his hand. "Simply put, I have been promised employment in California. In addition, I'll be given a large tract of land."

"I see."

"And this new company only accepts men who have capable wives." He narrowed his eyes in her direction. "From what you told me, you've worked at a factory since you were young."

"Very young, yes."

"And you will continue to work, only this time it will be by cultivating crops and tending to livestock. Do you think you can do that?" he asked. "Or this whole venture will be for naught."

"I have never worked a farm before but I am willing to learn if it means the betterment of our lives together," she answered with a certain hopefulness that almost had him excited for the future.

"Good." He nodded his head and sat down at the front of the wagon. Sarah settled herself in the back along with most of Aaron's possessions.

For the first hour of travel, they rode in silence. The only sound that accompanied them were those of the wagon.

Then, they were joined by other members of the company ready to make the same trek.

The hours were slow to go by. Aaron felt himself dozing off at the reigns. His head kept dropping onto his chest before he woke himself up again. "Perhaps you'd want me to take over," Sarah suggested. "I couldn't help but notice that you keep falling asleep."

"I am fine," he insisted.

Despite his answer, she sat down beside him. "May I?"

He huffed.

"I just want to be clear – I am not here to replace your wife."

He looked over at her as if she had just sported three heads. "How...?"

"I saw your portrait above the fireplace. And given your reaction to Clarise's passing, I simply assumed," she explained. "I just wanted you to know that I will not try to take her place."

"Thank you." A certain sense of relief made it easier for him to breathe. "It's been six months but sometimes it feels like just yesterday. Some nights, I can still feel the warmth of her hand against mine..." His voice faded into the wind.

Sarah did not bother to console him with her words for she had never been very good at doing so. Instead, she rubbed his back and gave him the shoulder he needed to cry on.

***

That night, the caravan settled as a tight circle to protect against any outside threats. "How long will it take us to reach California?" Sarah asked as she cooked some canned beans over the fire. She added some spices to improve the flavor.

"Months," answered Aaron. "And it will not be easy."

"But so long as we are together, I know we will make it there," she said with a smile as she handed over his plate of food. Together, they sat on some crates, not saying a word.

Sarah took the time to look around at all the other couples. Most of them were affectionate towards one another. They whispered and laughed. Even in the moonlight, Sarah could see the sparkle in the eyes of her fellow womenfolk. She envied them as she glanced over at her husband. He didn't even bother to strike up a conversation with her.

This was not what she had expected when she decided to come to America. She had banked everything on the fact that this man would be a dream come true but she should have known better.

With this thought weighing in her stomach like a boulder, she abandoned her plate and wandered past the perimeter of the caravan. There, the moonlight was a little brighter, casting everything in a silver sheen.

She followed a dirt path for a while, eventually coming across a body of water. The surface was so still that it functioned as a mirror. She leaned forward and considered her own reflection. What was it about her that made her so difficult to love? Everywhere she turned, people rejected her. First, her mother. And now, her own husband.

She pitied him, yes. She could only imagine how difficult it was to lose a loved one, but, at the same time, she hardly thought it fair what he was doing to her. Why marry if love wasn't to be a factor? She hugged herself, trying to come to terms with what her life had become.

Snap.

She turned around but saw nothing. She shrugged it off and bent towards the water. It was cold against her palms as she scooped it up and brought it to her lips. The drink invigorated her. Perhaps Aaron was not ready to love her at the current moment but that didn't stop him from loving her in the future. Sarah had to keep that hope alive.

Snap!

This time, the sound was louder. Her heart quickened as her instincts told her that something was wrong. Slowly, she pivoted on her heels. Her eyes nearly bugged right out of her head when she saw a giant wolf emerge from the tree line. He stalked forward, yellow eyes shining like oil lamps.

Sarah shuffled backward only to fall.

The wolf jumped forward, nearly upon her.

Other emerged from the thicket, following their alpha.

Frozen with fear, there was nothing she could do. Even screaming had become impossible as her throat clamped shut.

Is this my fate? she wondered. *To come to America only to be eaten by wolves?* She squeezed her eyes shut as the predators came nearer and nearer.

This is the end, she thought as the animals snarled in bloodthirsty preparation.

Chapter 5

Aaron finished his plate of beans when he finally realized that his wife was missing. He looked all around but could not see her anywhere. With a sigh, he checked the wagon but she was not there either.

Where could she have gone –

That thought was quickly interrupted by the sound of a wolf's howl.

His eyes widened as something told him that his new wife was in danger. His instincts took over as he grabbed his rifle and ran towards the sound.

He reached the lake and found his wife cowering in fear, the wolves readying themselves for an attack.

Fearing he might lose yet another wife, he was quick to fire. The bullet only barely grazed the animal's thick pelt. Blood soaked through to his fire but it was not enough to stop the predator.

The pack turned their attention towards the threat.

Aaron struggled to reload his gun. It was jammed. In the time that it took him, the wolves had already made their attack. The alpha tore at his arm while the others nipped at the rest of his body.

He screamed with pain as it burned through his every inch.

Seeing that the wolves were going to tear him apart, Sarah summoned all the courage she could find and managed to rise to her feet. With a rock in hand, she bashed it over the animal's skull, disorienting him.

Furious, the alpha snapped in her direction but Aaron deflected the attack. Once again, the animal snuck his teeth into Aaron's flesh. He cursed.

The wolf shook his head from side to side like he planned on ripping Aaron's arm right from the socket.

I have to do something! Sarah looked around and saw Aaron's rifle on the ground. She had never used a gun before but right now that didn't matter for if she waited any longer, she was sure to become a window.

She pushed down on the trigger and the kickback was enough to send her flying. At the same time, the bullet pierced through the wolf's head, killing it.

The other wolves whimpered before running off, tail between their legs.

Sarah dropped the gun and rushed to her husband's side. "Oh..." There was blood everywhere and she didn't quite know what to do about it.

"You saved me," he whispered despite the weakness he felt. "Why?"

"Because you are my husband," she said as she took his hand in hers. "And I do not want to lose you just like you did not want to lose your wife."

Aaron lifted up his hand then and cupped her cheek against his palm. "I'm sorry..." was all he managed to say before the darkness rolled over him.

***

Sarah drove the wagon the following morning. Luckily, the animals were well trained and knew to follow the others. All she had to do was keep her hands on the reigns.

Around midday, they stopped to rest. Sarah checked on her husband. She dressed his wounds and prayed for a miracle but his fever seemed to be getting worse and worse. At this rate, he was bound to perish and she would be left all alone – again.

Tears stung at the corners of her eyes. She knew better than to shed them. She needed to stay strong for the sake of her husband. He needed her and she wasn't about to let him down.

But the thought of being abandoned kept haunting her. "Please... don't leave me," she whispered.

As she always did whenever she was nervous, she fiddled with her rosary beads. The cross hung low, nearly brushing against his chest.

"I beg of you God. This man might not be the loving husband I had been looking for but he is still *mine* and I his. I do not want to part with him so soon. I don't even truly know who he is." She buried her head against his chest.

A second later, she felt his hand on the top of her head, fingers weaving through her hair.

She straightened out, eyes wide. "Aaron, you're awake!"

"So I am," he said. "And I heard what you said – the prayers you whispered." He struggled to right himself but he did not have the strength to do so on his own. Sarah had to help him and even then, he panted with the exertion. "And I want to apologize. It was not fair of me to marry you for my own selfish reasons without considering what you might need as well."

"All I need is for you to stay here with me."

Aaron did not understand. "Why are you so fond of me when I have treated you with nothing but coldness?"

"Because I am scared of being alone," she admitted. "I grew up in an orphanage because my mother did not want to keep me. She left me at their doorstep and there I lived until I turned 18. No one ever bothered to adopt me. Meanwhile, all my friends were whisked away to happy homes."

Aaron's heart became heavy as he listened to her story.

"And I do not expect you to pity me. All I ask is that you do not cast me aside as all others have."

He wrapped his uninjured arm around her. "It will be difficult for me to be the husband you deserve. My past is a blight to my present. And my wife's passing still hangs heavy in the air but I believe, with time, I can grow to love you, too."

Sarah cried with joy. "That is all I could ever ask of you."

He pulled her away slightly so he could lean into those soft lips of hers. This time, he actually kissed her. That sweetness of her soul simmered to the surface and broke down the walls he had built around his heart, hoping to protect it from future upsets. But to live is to love and to love is make oneself vulnerable.

So, he gave in to his emotions and held her even closer. Perhaps he deserved a second chance and perhaps Abigail would forgive him for moving on.

Epilogue

A few years later.

The wind howled against the windows, coating it with a thick layer of snow.

Sarah tried to look through it in hopes of spotting her husband coming up the path but all she saw was a sea of white. For the millionth time, she checked the time. It was getting late – very late.

It was unusual for her husband to take this long. Had something happened? Had the snow left him stranded somewhere?

Unable to wait any longer, she dressed in her warmest clothes and braved the elements. The wind was cruel against her cheeks. The air was so frigid it was difficult to breathe. Still, she continued forward, following the path that her husband took every morning. However, this task soon became impossible for everything was covered in a blanket of white. Sarah turned around, trying to determine her surroundings but it was hard to tell things apart.

Worry gripped at her heart as she pictured herself freezing to death. Already, she could feel the chill penetrating into her bones. She shivered, teeth chattering together. If she felt this way then she could only imagine what her husband must be going through.

"Aaron!" she called but her voice was muted by the roaring of the wind. "Aaron!" She tried again but to no avail.

Her fingers had turned numb.

Suddenly, she spotted something in the distance and ran in its direction. She stumbled a few times as her dress became heavy with snow. It became a chore to breathe. Once again, she had pushed herself too far. Her mind became foggy with the lack of oxygen. She toppled over, becoming buried by the fluff.

"Sarah!" She heard her husband but she could not respond. Her head felt like it was going to pop at my moment.

Aaron quickened to his wife and pulled her out of the snowbank to find that her skin had turned a terrifying blue tinge. "Breathe," he prompted. "Sarah, I need you to breathe for me." He held her by the shoulders and guided her through the rhythm. "Inhale – exhale. That's it."

Sarah managed to calm herself down.

"There." He kissed the top of her head with relief. "Now, what are you doing out here?"

"I came looking for you." Aaron was moved by the dedication of his wife. She was always thinking of him before she thought of herself. Sometimes, he did not understand how he had managed to deserve such a woman when he had been nothing but cold to her at the beginning of their marriage. Still, he wasn't about to complain.

She wasn't a replacement for Abigail but a whole new part of his life that he had learned to cherish.

"Come," he said as he wrapped his arm around her shoulders and guided her home. There, he added some wood to the fire.

They stripped out of their wet clothing and warmed themselves against the flames. "I never asked how she died," Sarah whispered.

Aaron stopped and stared into the distance. "She died of illness. I called on nearly every doctor in town but none of them were able to help her." His shoulders sagged. "I had to watch her die, bit by bit."

Sarah took his hand and squeezed it. "I can't even imagine."

"I suppose that's one reason why I tried to keep you at arm's length. I was afraid that if I learned to love another, I would go through the same heartache. I just couldn't bear the thought of having to say goodbye a second time." He turned to look at his wife and held her face in his hands. "But it has become impossible to keep from loving you."

Their lips came together in a soul-warming kiss. It radiated through Sarah's entire body until it felt like there was a fire burning through her core. She melted against it as the feeling lifted her up.

Aaron tightened his grip and pulled her onto his lap. There, he laced his fingers through her hair.

Sarah shivered with delight. She had always enjoyed the way he played with her hair.

The kiss became impossible to hold as Sarah's breath failed her. She pulled away, panting.

"Are you okay?" he asked, eyes painted with concern.

"More than okay," she answered. "I'm with you." She rested her head on his chest and listened to the steady beating of his heart. "When I dreamt of coming to America, this was never what I thought it would be."

"So, do you regret answering my ad?"

"Not at all. I quite enjoy tending to the farm. It's much more rewarding than working at a factory. I get to reap everything I sow."

Aaron nodded. "It isn't quite a life of glamor but it's a modest one."

"And I don't mind that so long as we always stay together." She laced their fingers together and felt like she was coming together with that missing puzzle piece. As she leaned forward, their foreheads met. She could smell the tobacco on his breath.

He smiled. "I promise. I will not abandon you like the others." His words were whispered against her ear. "And, even if something were to happen and one of us had to leave... well, it would all be worth it because our time spent together is something I would never trade away, not even for the world."

Sarah felt like her heart was melting. She smiled and their eyes locked together. She wouldn't mind gazing into their blue depths for the rest of her eternity.

"I love you." Despite being married for three years, it was the first time he had spoken those words. Each time he had attempted it, they had become lodged at the back of his throat. Now, by the warmth of the fire, they simply spilled from his lips.

"I love you, too," she whispered as she leaned into him, causing them both to fall over onto the carpet. She laughed as he tickled her sides.

Aaron was taken aback by her beauty and the joys of learning to love all over again.

TAINTED SPRING

NICOLE PORTER

<u>Chapter 1</u>

"I'll kill you Abigail, I swear it!" Collin yelled.

From the kitchen pantry, Abigail and her daughter, Barbara, trembled together. Every few seconds Abigail squeezed her daughter's hand.

They knew better than to make a sound. Being caught by Collin in one of his rages meant being hit. Or worse.

They'd never seen him this angry.

"Where is it Abigail?" he thundered, his black beard trembling with every word.

He smashed a pan to the floor, and started ripping open cupboards in search of his whisky.

Cupboard after cupboard was torn open. Abigail and Barbara exchanged a tear-filled look. They knew it was only a matter of time.

He flung open the pantry door and they screamed, rushing out. Barbara got away, ran to hide in the barn. But Abigail didn't have a chance. She was Collin's intended target, after all.

Grabbing Abigail by the wrists, Collin flung her to the floor.

"I said where is it?"

Abigail spoke to the wood floor, splintered from another one of his rages.

"It's not permitted. It's against the Ordnung."

He grabbed her by the bun, wrenched her head up to his face.

"You think I care? Women don't understand what hard work is really like."

He shoved her back to her hands and knees.

"You're a fool, Abigail. Always have been, always will be."

Grabbing her by the bun, he wrenched her up again.

"Now tell me – where is it?"

Abigail was sobbing so hard that Collin couldn't make out her first answer at all.

He shook her.

"What did you say?"

"I poured it out. It isn't right – the drinking."

Collin threw her back to the floor.

"Dumb woman."

He kicked her.

"Thinking you know better. You have no idea what I'm dealing with. I need it."

He kicked her again. And again. And again.

Abigail gasped out pleas, cries for him to stop, but his foot seemed detached from him, it kicked on and on, as she rolled to and fro like a rag doll. He only stopped when she fell still.

—

Abigail awoke to a cool cloth being pressed to her forehead. It was so dark she couldn't see anything, though she didn't have to. She knew. It was Barbara.

A low moan escaped Abigail's lips, and this time it was Barbara who squeezed her hand.

"It's ok Mom. It's going to be ok."

Abigail fell silent. She didn't have the heart to tell her daughter that she didn't believe her.

"I love you so much," Abigail said, forcing herself up to a sitting position and embracing Barbara, "More than you know."

It was true. Only her love for her daughter had kept her locked in this loveless, abusive relationship.

"It won't happen again," Abigail said, smoothing Barbara's flyaway hair, "I promise."

She meant it. Never again would she try to stop Collin from drinking. Even though whiskey made his rages worse, getting rid of it was more dangerous.

Barbara yawned.

Painstakingly, Abigail rose, each of her limbs groaning protest.

She had to get Barbara to bed. She didn't want her falling asleep in class again. The poor girl had suffered enough as it was.

Taking Barbara's hand, whispering "Time for bed", Abigail brought Barbara to her room. Then, folding the patchwork quilt just under Barbara's chin, Abigail tucked her into bed. She stroked her daughter's hair as she sang the old lullaby she had sung when she was a baby: "Sleep, my baby, sleep!

Your Daddy's tending the sheep.

Your Mommy's taken the cows away.

Won't come home till break of day.

Sleep, my baby, sleep!"

By the end of the first verse, Barbara had nodded off.

Abigail watched her for a minute: the peaceful rising and falling of her chest with every breath. Sometimes she wondered how something so good could have come from her and Collin. She wondered if her daughter would look so peaceful if she knew what her mother was about to do.

As Abigail walked out of the room, she reasoned with herself. She had no choice. It had been weeks since she had been alone with him. And especially after today's incident she needed to see him or she was going to go crazy.

Abigail tiptoed out of the house and didn't resume a normal tread until she was off their property and on his. Even then, every few steps, she looked around, squinting worriedly through the dark.

There was no need to wonder what would happen to her if she were caught. The whole community would shun her. She would never see Barbara again.

As she neared, Barbara saw a light on in the front porch of the house. As if he knew.

Abigail smiled, then shuddered.

Maybe her cries of pain had been so loud that he had heard them all the way over here.

Abigail knocked four times then once, and then again, four times then once. Nothing happened. Abigail peered in the front door window, but all she could see was more darkness.

What if something had happened to him? What if he wasn't coming at all?

But then the door swung open.

"Ike," Abigail whispered as the face she had come to so love brightened upon seeing her.

As soon as she stepped inside into the light, however, his face fell.

"Not again," Ike said, a break in his voice.

Abigail avoided his gaze, as it slid from her bruised arms to her ripped apron. If she caught his eye, she would start sobbing right there.

"It was my fault. I hid the whiskey. I should've known better."

Anger flashed in Ike's eyes. He stepped forward to seize her hands, stopping himself at the last second.

"That's ridiculous, and you know it. Abigail, please, we should go to Jonah. Tell him about how Collin drinks, the way he beats you."

Abigail's said nothing, kept her gaze on the floor. Ike gestured into the sitting room, to the same plaid armchair as usual.

Abigail went over and flopped down on it. When she glanced over at Ike, he was still waiting for an answer.

So, with a sigh, she said: "You know Jonah would never believe us. Collin is his son. All that would happen is that you and I would be excommunicated, and I'd never see Barbara again."

For a minute Ike stayed frozen in place with his face turned away, as if trying to refuse what had been said. But after a minute, he sighed too, and sat down on the armchair next to her.

"You're right, of course." - he sat up straighter and shot her a smile - "Despite the circumstances, I'm glad to see you."

Abigail spoke to her hands; it had been so long, she felt shy to look Ike in the eye.

"Words can't express how happy seeing you has made me."

She cast him a sidelong glance. Seeing the goofy grin her words had brought to his face, she couldn't hold back a smile of her own.

Ike leapt up.

"Almost forgot, I got you something."

He returned with a small knitted flower that he placed in Abigail's palm.

"So I can be with you always."

Abigail raised the little red and yellow thing to her face, inhaled its pine scent, the pine scent that was Ike's, and smiled.

"Thank you."

Ike sat back down, his smile resting on Abigail contentedly.

"I know you don't like me saying it, Abigail, but I know we'll be together. Don't ask me how, I just know."

Abigail looked at him longingly, wishing his smile could become hers, wishing she could still believe him. But it had been nine years now. Nine years of longing looks and no physical contact, of nighttime visits and daytime stolen glances. Nine years of nothing.

Maybe in the beginning she could have believed Ike. After all, he had bought land right beside Collin's, started working within the church to modernize their doctrine – to allow exceptions to the no divorce rule for the case of immoral spouses.

He had remained a steadfast bachelor all the while – much to the surprise of the community – and nothing else had changed either. The minister and the church were set in their ways, while Collin only grew more angry and violent.

Abigail placed her hand beside his on the arm of her armchair, their hands one thin block of plaid apart. She smiled and closed her eyes.

Yes, for all Ike's talk, she knew this was it. Here, now, these would be her happiest moments, stolen seconds with a man who was not hers, but who was good and kind. Who loved her.

It seemed only a second later that Ike said: "Abigail– get up – quick! It's almost light outside."

Abigail jumped up and raced to the door.

"Goodbye Ike!" she said over her shoulder, "I can't thank you enough. For everything."

"Wait!" said Ike, running after her.

At the door, he pressed something in her hand, paused as if to say something more, then opened the door, gesturing for her to go.

"There's no time – Collin could be up any minute. Hurry!"

As she ran down the road, kicking up dust as she went, Abigail looked at what was in her hand.

The knitted flower. She brought it to her nose, inhaled deep and smiled.

Whatever came today, she could handle it. As long as Collin hadn't woken up yet.

By the time she reached her house, the rooster had started crowing. Abigail could hardly breathe she was running so fast. She threw herself through the door and then –

"Abigail?"

Abigail froze.

Chapter 2

It was Collin. His footsteps pounded down the steps – angrily?

"Yes?"

His face looked sad, sorry.

"I'm sorry Abigail. I overreacted last night. There's just some things you don't know, is all."

Abigail kept her gaze on his feet, his scuffed-up shoes that had kicked her last night and would kick her again.

She nodded, played her part in the charade that had been acted out a hundred times before.

Collin strode past her into the kitchen.

"What – no breakfast?"

Abigail glared at his back.

"I'm sorry. I'll get some cornmeal mush started right away," she said and got to work.

She took several ears of field corn out of the pantry, removed the husks, and started cutting. The whup-whup-whup of her knife was a welcome outlet for her anger.

She hated Collin. Would she ever be free of him? If only something would happen to him, if only he were struck by a horse or had some sort of an accident.

Abigail froze, looking at herself in the glint of the knife. No, no that wasn't right. She wouldn't wish that even on Collin. She would only pray that through God's grace he would come to see the error of his ways.

As Abigail moved on to the next ear, after her first three whup-whups, there was a crash, then a shout.

Abigail ran outside to find Collin splayed out on the ground, an upturned wheelbarrow beside him. The wheelbarrow's dirt had fallen on him and he was half-submerged in it.

Abigail ran up to him and kneeled beside him.

"Collin are you ok?"

Collin's mouth was locked into a snarl, his eyes blinking rapidly, looking at something beyond Abigail.

"Collin?" – she shook him – "Collin?"

And then he fell still.

"No," Abigail said, unable to believe what she was seeing.

"No, no, no," she said, shaking Collin, over and over again.

"Mom?" Barbara called from the doorway, then, kneeling beside her: "Mom? Dad?"

Abigail was still locked in motion, tears spilling down her face onto Collin's still open-eyed, snarling one.

"No, no, no," she moaned, "What have I done? What have I-"

And then together, she and Barbara shook him, the man who had left them behind, wronged them beyond belief, the man they still needed now anyway.

When after a minute or ten, Barbara asked: "Mom, what should we do?", the realization struck Abigail like a slap to the face.

Collin was gone. Dead. She had to get help.

"Wait here Barbara," she told the girl, whose pink face was a river of tears.

It didn't take long for Abigail to run to the church, it was the land on the other side of her house after all. As soon as she ran through the church's front doors she knew something was wrong.

Hannah was sitting erect on a chair in the entrance. On seeing Abigail, her thick eyebrows lowered so much they nearly made her eyes disappear altogether.

"Abigail," her cool voice said as she stood up.

The words tumbled out of Abigail: "It's Collin, he fell, he – you have to come Hannah. Is Jonah here?"

Hannah's mouth drew into a thin line, her hands clenched into bony fists.

"What have you done to my son?" she hissed, before sweeping off into the chapel.

She returned a moment later with Jonah, and they all took off for Abigail's house.

In the grass out front, beside the upturned wheelbarrow, Barbara was in the same position as before. Ike's body, on the other hand, to Abigail looked somehow even worse: his eyes were open wider, while his mouth was even more of a distorted snarl, as if raging against what had happened.

Abigail watched with shaking legs as Hannah and Jonah, bent over their son's body, wept. She held Barbara's hand, which was wet from her daughter's tears or her own; she couldn't tell. She squeezed it.

"Barbara," Hannah said after a few minutes, rising to her feet, "Barbara, come with me."

The old woman held out a pale hand, which was also wet with tears.

"Abigail," Jonah said, rising just as Abigail was about to reply, "Come talk with me."

His tone was devoid of all emotion, his blue eyes gray. Hannah, however, was looking at Abigail like she had strangled Collin with her bare hands. Something was going on.

"Abigail," Jonah said softly, and that was when Abigail understood that none of this was a choice.

Abigail nodded, hugged Barbara goodbye and watched as Hannah stalked back towards the church with her daughter's little hand trapped in her bony grip.

"Shall we?" Jonah said, gesturing to the house. They walked in through the kitchen, the remnants from before the accident strangely chilling: the half-cut-up corn, the still-ajar pantry door. Abigail looked down: even her apron was still on. And to think, less than an hour ago, last time she was there, it hadn't happened yet.

Jonah sat on a chair and gestured for Abigail to do the same.

"Hannah saw you last night," Jonah said as soon as she sat down.

Abigail knew then that it was all over.

Still, she tried to get the words out, tried to get her say in, before what Jonah said made his decision final.

"Jonah – please – I swear to you, there has been nothing untoward.. I have always been faithful to Collin, despite..."

She let the sentence trail off, didn't say despite what; Jonah and Hannah had always been blind when it came to their only son.

Jonah didn't even glance at Abigail; he spoke to the cut-up corn, as if it was more worthy of his attention.

"I don't know much about much, but I do know that this doesn't look good, that the Bishop will have to be informed. And now that my son has died..." Jonah gave her a long, hard look – "This doesn't look good at all."

"Jonah, I-"

He held up his hand.

"For the time being, I think we can all agree that it's best that Barbara stay with Hannah and me-"

"Jonah, please-"

He held up his hand again, this time something of Collin's dying snarl on his face.

"I wasn't finished. In the meantime, we will be bringing this to the attention of the community, to see what they have to say. Ike has always been a good parishioner. If he has engaged in anything untoward, Hannah and I have no doubt that it is because he has been seduced into it by you. From the start, you have not behaved as a wife should."

Jonah rose.

"You may find that you will be excommunicated in the next week or so for what you have done. May God forgive you Abigail."

Abigail rose.

"Jonah," she said, "Please..."

But he strode through the door and away, as if he hadn't heard her at all.

<u>Chapter 3</u>

After Jonah had left, Abigail watched the door swing in and out, in and out, stared at it for a while, as if Jonah might come back. As if there was the smallest chance that things would be made right.

Finally Abigail directed her gaze to the chopped-up corn bits, which was what she'd be soon: cut off, alone.

A great tiredness descended upon her, and she made her way upstairs and collapsed into bed.

Abigail awoke crying once, a hundred times. Each time she couldn't bear to get up, and rolled to the other side, lay there until she fell back asleep again.

Finally, when she couldn't lie down for another second, Abigail got up and stumbled out into the hallway. According to the clock, a day had passed, maybe two.

She stumbled out onto the street, hardly knew where she was headed. She couldn't go to Ike, not now, probably not ever. She only realized her destination when a collie scampered across the street.

Mercy. Of course. Her collie was named Abraham. Mercy was all Abigail had left now. They'd been friends since Abigail was a kid, Mercy wouldn't abandon her now.

The further Abigail walked, the less sure she became, however. No one would look at her. First were Noah and Miriam, who crossed to walk on the other side of the street. Further down the road, Patience kept her fiery gaze locked on her feet as she passed.

Abigail used to love this long walk to Mercy's farm, which was situated at the edge of the community's land, seeing all her friends as she walked. Now, she wasn't sure she could make it at all.

Further down, on a house porch, Abigail passed Otto and Roman, their conversation stopping as abruptly as if she'd cut it with scissors herself.

The rest of the way, Abigail kept her gaze on her feet. They were bare, dirty and calloused.

Like most women, she went shoeless in the summer to avoid wearing out her shoes. Her left pinky toe was still bent funny from when Collin had slammed his boot down on her foot.

As soon as Mercy saw Abigail, she walked out to meet her.

"Abigail," she said.

Mercy's face was white and though her lips had spoken Abigail's name, her eyes didn't seem to be seeing her.

"Mercy," Abigail said, stepped forward, for a hug.

Mercy stepped back, looked over her shoulder. Samuel was standing on the porch, watching them.

"I heard what happened," Mercy said.

Abigail shook her head.

"No, Mer, no, none of what they're saying is true. Jonah's death was an accident, I don't know what happened. Sure, he was mean – you knew that, but I didn't do anything to him. I swear it."

Mercy nodded, though her eyes still looked through Abigail.

"And Ike..." Abigail began.

Mercy looked over her shoulder to Samuel again.

"I think you should go, Abigail."

"But Mercy," Abigail said, her eyes searching her friend's face for some uncertainty, some sadness, anything.

But Mercy looked at her like a stranger and turned her back on her and left.

Abigail stood there for a minute, her eyes burning with tears, at the pain of it, at the humiliation. Seth and Sara were passing, staring with that same hard look all of them wore now – as if she had been excommunicated already.

Abigail wiped her eyes and exhaled. Then, she ran.

She wasn't going to give any of them the satisfaction of seeing her cry. She ran without seeing – her vision blinded by tears and the dust her feet were kicking up, without hearing – the rasp of her breath and pounding of her feet louder than anything else.

When she got back to her house, Jonah was waiting in the kitchen, sitting on the same chair he had been in before.

"Abigail," he said, when she walked in, "Sit down."

Abigail shook her head.

"Tell me," she said in a quavering voice, though she already knew, "Tell me Jonah."

"The Bishop has been informed of the situation and is investigating the case. In the meantime, the community has made a decision."

Jonah gestured to the chair again, and, in a voice devoid of feeling, said: "Are you sure you don't want to sit down?"

Abigail shook her head again. It was the only thing she was sure of: that she would not take whatever he had to say sitting down.

"You are to be excommunicated pending the outcome," Jonah said, and Abigail found that the only thing she really did need now, was a chair.

She staggered to the counter, grabbed onto the edge for support.

"Barbara will of course stay with us in the meantime," he said, rising, his task done.

Abigail whirled around.

"No – Jonah – please, please, I'm begging you-"

She seized the edge of his coat. He looked at her, his mouth rising into Collin's same death snarl.

"Goodbye Abigail," he said, wrenching his coat free and striding out the door.

Abigail rushed after him.

"Please Jonah – I have nowhere, nothing – Collin left me nothing you know, nothing – and Barbara, my daughter, my dear sweet daughter – please, I'm begging you."

Jonah stopped, turned to face her.

"The community's decision is final."

Even as he continued on, Abigail staggered after him, her feet slipping and her entire body falling into the same dirt no one had cleaned up since Collin's death.

There, belly-down in the dirt, Abigail raised her head and screamed into the sky.

Then she screamed again and again, until her voice was hoarse and she let her head drop into the dirt. There was nothing to do now, except lay there and die.

—

Abigail awoke shaking. She squinted open her eyes to see blinding sun—then closed them again.

"Abigail are you alright?"

At Ike's voice, Abigail opened her eyes again and accepted the hand that was offered her. She was pulled to a seated position, and Ike sat on the ground across from her.

"I heard what happened."

Abigail looked away, to her house. The front door was still open.

"You shouldn't be here Ike."

"What does it matter now, Abigail? They've excommunicated you unfairly. This is wrong. From the start you've been the victim and now you're being blamed as the criminal."

The front door to her house was swinging softly in the breeze. Abigail shook her head, still unable to bear looking at Ike.

"I've been a bad wife, a bad mother. I've betrayed Collin in my thoughts – and in my actions. And now I'm being punished for it."

Ike seized her hand. Abigail's eyes fluttered to his as she drew back. Never before had they touched each other like that.

"Betrayed? Abigail, if anyone has been the betrayer, it's me. I'm the one who has been pursuing you from the start – at the beginning you were the one who begged me to leave you be – don't you remember? This is my fault, and I'm going to make this right."

Ike stood up, and offered his hand to Abigail. Without taking his hand, Abigail wobbled her way upright.

"You have more faith in the community then they warrant, I'm afraid," she said.

But Ike's head was already turned towards the church, his tanned face hopeful, his blue eyes clear.

When he turned back to Abigail and clasped her hand once more, his mouth was set in a determined line.

"I swear it to you Abigail. I said it once and I'll say it again, we will be together. I will make this right."

Abigail said nothing more, her gaze on her own muddied feet and front. Ike's gaze was still on the church – he couldn't see it. See that she was muddied beyond cleaning.

—

Ike walked Abigail back to her house. He cleaned up the kitchen – finally throwing out those horrible rotting corn kernels, made her some tea. And then he left. As he went, he cast a look around the darkened room, the night casting everything into ominous-looking shadows.

"Mark my words Abigail, this house will be different by the time I come back. Soon, everything will be different."

Abigail nodded, managing a half-hearted smile as he left. She looked at the shadow of the pantry, the door still open. She sure hoped Ike was right. If not, there would be nothing left for her.

—

Abigail waited and waited. She couldn't sleep before she had found out. She couldn't bear waking up with the crushing weight of her excommunication upon her.

But the wait seemed to stretch on forever. Abigail found herself nodding off, and the next thing she knew her front door was opening.

Ike was back, except it was still dark out, and the house was the same.

He said the words Abigail had known he would:

"I'm sorry, Abigail."

And then he said: "It's not hopeless, however, the community said they'd let me address everyone and have another vote on it tomorrow. I know I can convince them Abigail, I'm sure of it."

It was too dark for Abigail to see Ike's face, but the hope of his words got lost in the shadows all around her.

"Abigail?" Ike asked.

"Yes?"

"I spoke to my brother at the church too. He was Collin's closest friend. He hasn't told anyone yet, but Collin had a heart condition. It made Collin stressed all the time, maybe even made him so stressed that he drank."

Abigail nodded, slowly, the revelation hitting her as a blow to the chest. All this time, and Collin never told her. And to think that she had judged her poor sick husband so harshly.

Ike continued: "Philip never told anyone because Collin made him swear not to. He was too proud. Philip still doesn't want to tell anyone, but I know can convince him."

Abigail nodded again, this one only a hollow repetition of the first.

"I should go now," Ike said, "They're going to be watching the two of us closely. I'm sure Hannah and Jonah are eager to discredit me. But there's hope Abigail!"

"Yes," Abigail said.

He clasped her hand again, and, as he left, with the other she squeezed the knitted flower tightly.

It was for the best that Ike didn't know, didn't realize just how doomed the situation was. He had never been there when it was just her and Philip, so he'd never seen the way his brother looked at her, never seen the suspicious hatred in his little eyes.

Now that Abigail was alone she pressed the little flower to her check and broke down sobbing.

—

This time when Abigail woke up it was still dark, but she was moving. Abigail sat up, and was shoved back down.

When she opened her eyes she saw only darkness. She tossed back and forth but was kicked in the back over again and over again until she fell still. Pain still ratcheting down her back, Abigail let out a soundless moan. Her lips quivered under the gag. Her arms and legs were bound. Her eyes were blindfolded. She was in some sort of bag. All she could do was roll – and not even that, for she would be kicked. No, all Abigail could really do was wait in terror for what was to come.

Chapter 4

While her body lay bound and useless, Abigail's terrors were given free reign. Who was doing this to her? She could hear the clop of hooves so it had to be someone from the community. Hannah? Jonah? Was the whole community in on it? Was God finally doling out the punishment she so justly deserved?

Forgetting herself, Abigail crumpled herself in a ball – and was kicked again – sending a new stream of tears down her cheek.

Where were they taking her? Were they going to throw her in some ditch – leave her there to die? Or worse - throw her in the lake, where her body would probably be rotted to unrecognizability before it was ever found?

Abigail shuddered at the thought.

Then again, would being thrown out of the community be any worse? No, Abigail realized, being thrown out into the outside world would be as good as a death sentence. She couldn't survive out there.

At some point, the horses' hooves fell silent. Then came the sound of footsteps, of unzipping. Abigail was unrolled and untied. Only her blindfold and gag were left on.

"Don't move," said a gruff voice she didn't recognize, "If you move in the next 5 minutes, I'll shoot you."

She was kicked once. Then she heard footsteps, then the clop of horses' hooves. Then silence.

Abigail wondered how she was supposed to be sure that five minutes had passed. She counted to a hundred in her head a few times.

When something landed on her and started cawing, Abigail shook, pulling off the blind and then the gag. A crow flew off, away into the gray sky.

Below the gray sky was more gray: she was in some concrete place. Abigail pinched herself, closed her eyes once more. But there was no escaping it – she was awake.

At her feet were the remains of what she had been tied and transported in: a large black duffel bag and several pieces of rope.

Abigail stared at them for a minute, trembling.

So the community had done it – not only excommunicated Abigail from her home, but actually physically removed her from it. If the way whoever had taken Abigail treated her was any indication, returning wouldn't be safe. Now, Abigail would never see her daughter or Ike again.

Abigail thought back to Rumspringa – the time when she had been a teenager and allowed on trips into the city to explore the outside world. Now, the knowledge she had gained on these trips would be her lifeline.

Abigail began walking towards a road she could see in the distance. Hopefully she could get a car to stop, tell her which way the nearest city or town was.

Now she had nothing– no money, only the muddied and now torn clothes on her back. That and the knowledge that cities in the outside world had places for people who had nothing – she'd heard about them– "shelters" they were called.

If she made it to one of those, maybe she would be alright. At least for now, for the next few days. Any farther ahead she didn't have the energy to think about.

As Abigail walked, she smiled at the gray sky.

As long as it didn't rain, it would be fine like this – perfect even. The sun would make her too hot, the dark too cold. The stretching of her legs felt good. Abigail was still on the verge of tears, but crying wouldn't help anyone – least of all herself.

She took out Ike's flower from her brassiere, where the tiny knitted thing had been hidden, and squeezed as she walked. It was almost as if Ike was there with her.

When the first car passed, Abigail was too much in her own thoughts to notice until it sped right by.

Abigail ran after it, waving, but she was too late.

After that, she stayed on her guard, listened carefully to the sounds of the road. And, when the next car drove near, she was ready.

She turned around to face the coming black Honda and waved wildly, leaning out into the road. She knew the spectacle she have been making with her clothes and gestures, but she didn't care. She had to get a car to stop.

The black Honda, however, zoomed right by, all its occupants on their phones.

Abigail sighed, and continued her trek.

After her first failure, she had three more cards drive by. The latest was the most infuriating, with its young female driver and her male companion gaping at Abigail uselessly.

Finally, after Abigail engaged in her most determined waving bout yet, a silver minivan pulled over, and an Einstein-haired man peered out of a window.

"Please, where is the nearest city?" Abigail asked.

The window descended, and the Einstein-haired man squinted at her.

"Waterloo is four hours or so that way," he said.

He swept his hand down the long expanse of road that, with the tone of his description, seemed to stretch to infinity.

"Thank you," Abigail said.

She turned away with a sigh.

"Would you like a ride?" a female voice asked.

Abigail turned back to see a white-haired woman behind the man, smiling kindly at her. Abigail stared at them for a minute. They looked like good people.

"Ok," she said.

An older boy in the back seat swung open the door, and Abigail got in.

She sat down in the middle seat and soon found herself awash in conversation.

The Salisowells were kind and curious, but not pushy. They took her claim that she was "visiting the city" at face value, regaled her with stories of Waterloo's recent heritage train that took visitors through town.

It was with a sad longing the Abigail took in the couple's clasped hands in the front of the car, their wrinkled fingers entwined. Maybe life could have been different for her, if she hadn't met Collin.

At Abigail's request, they dropped her off at the train station, which was right in the city center and wished her well. She waved goodbye with the question of where the shelter was on her lips. She had gotten to know them too well, was too embarrassed to ask.

As the silver minivan pulled off, Abigail turned her attention to the train station, its platform flocked with passengers who were all staring at her. She had to get to the shelter as fast as she could.

Swallowing her pride, Abigail strode up to the ticket counter inside the station and asked the man where the nearest shelter was.

With a look of obvious distaste at her disheveled appearance, the man said "Corner of Metcalfe and Cumberland."

"Thank you," Abigail said, although the man had only increased her worries. Street names meant nothing to her.

However, as she was walking out, an older woman who had seen their exchange, spoke to her: "You are in search of the Waterloo mission – the shelter? I volunteer there on occasion. I have arrived early for my train. I can bring you to the mission now."

Abigail agreed, and the old woman led her out to the parking lot to a shiny maroon station wagon. Then, the old woman got in the driver's seat, Abigail got in the passenger's, and they were off.

The old woman chattered nonstop to Abigail, who sank into her seat gratefully. It was clear that the woman spoke merely for the act itself and no acknowledgement on the part of her listener was required.

It didn't take long before the maroon station wagon was pulling up to a red-bricked building with a group of scraggly-looking men outside it.

The woman waved to it, saying: "Here we are. Now, just remember what I told you and you'll do fine."

Then, with one final wave, she swept Abigail out of the car and sped away. It all happened so fast that Abigail didn't have time to ask what exactly she had to remember.

Abigail's heart sank as she took in the scraggly-looking men, who were leering at her. Whatever that old woman had told her, it had probably been important.

Chapter 5

Abigail hurried inside the shelter.

At the desk was a severe-looking woman with gigantic silver glasses.

"Yes?" the woman said, throwing a look up at Abigail, then back down at the papers she was writing on.

"I... I would like to stay here," Abigail said timidly.

"Sorry," the woman said, her eyes still on whatever she was writing, "No beds left."

"I don't think you understand," Abigail said slowly, "I have nowhere else to go."

The woman tossed up another look, this one resting on Abigail for a moment, as if she were surprised that she was still there.

"We run out of beds fast. You can come in tomorrow morning and reserve one first thing."

The woman's gaze transferred back to her papers.

"And until then?" Abigail asked.

The woman looked up at her coldly and adjusted her glasses.

Abigail turned and walked out. There was nothing left to do now. No hope left.

"Abigail!"

At the familiar voice, she froze.

That had been, and yet it couldn't be...

"Ike?"

The next thing Abigail knew she was seeing the beaming face of her love and being lifted by his embrace.

Amidst the scraggly-looking men's jeers and whoops, Abigail began laughing and crying herself.

"How did you ever find me?" she asked when Ike put her down.

Ike still spoke with an ear-to-eat grin: "I'd been watching your house, keeping an eye on you. So I saw when you were taken. They were too many of them and they weren't from our community. Hired maybe. Anyway, I followed them, but lost them on the highway. I kept questioning people on the road until I found someone who'd seen you. They told me the nearest town and when I got here, I went to the only place I could think of you going."

Abigail nodded, an ear-to-ear grin stuck on her face too.

Ike seized her hand and squeezed it, "We're going to make a life here, you and I Abigail. It's going to be one crazy life – but we're going to do it- together. We'll build a life here until their decision, and then, regardless, we'll find a way to get Barbara back."

Abigail squeezed his hand back, and looked to the sky. The sun was peeking out between the clouds.

I WOULD LIKE MY HEART BACK NOW

44

MONICA MANN

<u>December</u>

The service had been lovely as always but Hannah had been unable to concentrate, her mind bustling with dozens of thoughts. As she followed her fiancé's family from the home of one of the member and into the back area of their farm, she wrung her hands nervously.

"Hannah, are you unwell?" She jumped at the sound of Isaac's voice near her ear.

"Not at all! On the contrary, in fact," she replied, peering at him, confusion coloring her face. "What would make you ask such a thing?"

"You seemed not to be paying any attention whatsoever during the sermon. I believe the Bishop scowled at you at one moment." Shocked, Hannah paused in mid step to stare at her husband-to-be, abruptly holding up the line trekking through the field.

"You must be joking!" she cried and then saw the twinkle in Isaac's gentle hazel eyes.

"Perhaps I am but you must admit that your mind has been elsewhere today. What are you thinking about? I noticed the faraway look in your eye from my side of the room!" Hannah laughed and continued toward the barn where the Fisher family had arranged for lunch following their Sunday worship. The winter had been unseasonably warm and Hannah felt somewhat overdressed in her wool cloak. She wished for snow. It did not feel festive without snowflakes gracing the air.

"Well? What is it that plagues your thoughts? Are you reconsidering our marriage?" Again, Isaac's warm eyes lit up with laughter and Hannah grinned broadly at his jesting.

"Certainly not! I am simply concerned about Christmas," Hannah replied, her thoughts beginning to race once more. It was Isaac's turn to show confusion.

"What of Christmas? It is the loveliest time of year. Surely you can't be glum!"

"Not in the least," Hannah replied as they made their way into the spacious structure to join the rest of the congregation. "I am simply worried I have not prepared properly. I have made presents of all of the children and for my parents but I feel as though I have forgotten someone. Which brings me to the Christmas cards. I am always concerned that I have left out a family. Can you imagine how much embarrassment that would bring to us should I omit a single family? What's more is I set up the nativity scene in the front of our home and I cannot find one wise man and two angels. Now I suspect that Rachel has been playing with them but I have yet to find them and she denies knowing their whereabouts. I must have father whittle some for me or else it will be a disaster!"

Suddenly Hannah felt as though a huge weight had been lifted off her shoulders with the confession. Isaac burst into laughter.

"Oh, Hannah! The things which make you fret do amuse me endlessly. It is Christmastime, *liebchen*. It is not a time of worry and fret. That is for the English. We are only to give thanks and spend time with those dearest to us."

"I know, Isaac, but I cannot help wanting Christmas to be perfect! It is my favorite time of the year. And look! This year we haven't even any snow! It hardly seems proper to even set up a tree without the candlelight twinkling off the snow." Hannah pouted but immediately smiled as the truth of his words struck her. Of course he was right; this was not a time of stress. Their way was that of peace and order, not to be overshadowed by the trivialities which the outside word concerned themselves. It was what made the Amish community so special; the ability to block out the unnecessary and focus on the beauty of the basics in life. Hannah could not be happier. She and Isaac had become betrothed in February and their impending marriage was announced to the community in October as per tradition. They had plans to wed the following winter as per tradition and she could not have hoped for a better mate. Despite their engagement, Isaac continued to act as though they were newly enamored with one another, bequeathing her with beautiful flowers and penning poetry for her, words which made her warm to her soul. She was excited to begin her life with him. It seemed that the wedding was millennia away, not merely a year.

"Ah, Hannah, you may worry but your Christmas spirit is infectious," Bishop Philips told her, overhearing the last of their conversation. Blushing scarlet, Hannah turned to acknowledge him, bowing her head.

"Your sermon was well received today, Bishop," Hannah told him, trying to recover from her embarrassment. "It is a rare treat to hear you speak lately. I'm afraid we miss hearing your voice in service. I am pleasantly surprised you have joined us today."

"Unfortunately, I have had business in other districts as of late but I am happy to be back at home. I haven't had the opportunity to congratulate on your betrothal. Isaac, you have done well for yourself. The Yoder family is well respected in our district. Perhaps you will bless them with a son." The Bishop smiled at the couple.

"Not that the Yoder women are any less hard working than any of the men in our community. How is your family? I do not see your father here today," the Bishop continued, looking about, a sudden cloud covering his brown eyes. Hannah and Isaac followed his gaze. Hannah's mother, Ruth stood speaking with several other women while her sisters, Rachel and Miriam ran through the barn, playing a game of tag with some of the other children. As the three continued to look about, Hannah felt a stab of panic in her stomach. It was unheard of for her father, Mark to be absent from church services. She had spent the previous week in Isaac's district at a family member's home. Hannah had been slowly learning the workings of his father's farm at the insistence of Mark who thought it best she understood the complexities of her husband's land as much as possible. As Hannah's cousins resided in close proximity to Isaac's farm, the transition had been seamless and it allowed for their sweet courtship to continue uninterrupted. This also meant, however, that Hannah was not as informed as to the comings and goings of her own family. Brow furrowed, Hannah excused herself and hurried over to her mother, despite Isaac's reactionary hand on her arm to stop her.

"*Mamm*, where is *Daed*?" she whispered in her mother's ear urgently without preamble. Ruth gave Hannah a reproving look and politely exited the conversation in which she was involved.

"Mind your manners, Hannah!" Ruth Yoder chided her daughter.

"I'm sorry Mammi, I am just worried about him. It is unlike him to miss service. I can't recall one instance prior to this one in fact!" Hannah insisted. Seeing her oldest daughter's distress, Ruth's face softened.

"Your father was away at market in Pittsburgh over the weekend. He was expecting to be back last night but the weather turned so he must have been detained. He will likely be home when we return." Hannah exhaled with relief and returned to her fiancé and the Bishop where she reiterated what she had been told. A bell rang to indicate that the meal was about to be served and they all sat at the long tables set up in the middle of building. Yet as they bowed their heads and grace was said, once again, Hannah felt herself distracted by unstoppable thoughts. This time, however, they were not of snowfalls and wise men. Suddenly she her mind was focussed completely on the whereabouts of her father.

"I don't mind, Hannah but I cannot help but feel you are overreacting somewhat," Isaac informed her as they pulled their carriage toward the Yoder farm.

"He is my father. I must know that he is well, Isaac," Hannah replied.

"*Liebchen*, he has been going to market since well before you were born. I am sure he is well. You will see." Isaac smiled boyishly at her and encouraged the horses onward. Hannah felt an uncharacteristic smidgen of annoyance at his placation. She gave him a sidelong look but said nothing. She hoped he was right but some inherent sense told her something was amiss. Inclement weather or not, Mark Yoder would have been at worship. His devotion to God was his priority, probably above his own health and safety. Hannah knew her father. He would have risked riding in a blizzard to honor his commitment to the community. Her mother had arrived back from the Miller farm with Rachel and Miriam and the pale afternoon light was already becoming dark, forsaking dusk altogether.

"I do not see his wagon," Hannah mumbled as they pulled to a stop. Alarm growing in her chest, Hannah recognized the Bishop's carriage which was parked behind the modest house. Hannah did not wait for Isaac to escort her from her seat and instead was running up the front steps to toward the door. As she flew inside the house, she stopped in her tracks. Her mother was on her knees, surrounded by Rachel and Miriam, a look of shock upon their faces. Tears had slipped from their cheeks to the wood floor. Bishop Phillips stood, solemn faced at the base of the stairs, his hat in his hands, his lips pursed into a fine line. They did not need to speak. Hannah already knew.

January

"Hannah, Isaac came calling again," Miriam told her, pushing open the door to the bedroom where her sister sat brushing her long hair, placing it into sections for braiding. Hannah did not respond. Instead she continued to count the strokes, slowly, meticulously smoothing down the strands.

"Hannah? Hannah!" Miriam strode into the room and snatched the utensil from her sister's grip. The older girl looked up in surprise and instinctively grabbed it back.

"What is it?" she demanded, rising to her feet menacingly.

"Isaac was here," Miriam said again. "He would like you to contact him when you are well."

"I am well, thank you. I am simply busy. With *Daed* in the hospital, fighting for his life, someone needs to help *Mamm* run the farm, Miriam. I cannot up and run off to help him when Isaac has able bodied brothers there. What does he want from me?" Her words were like a torrent of venom and twelve-year-old Miriam stepped back, shocked at her tone.

"I believe that he wants to know if you're well, Hannah. I don't think he wants you to help him on the farm," she offered, timidly, tears filling her eyes. Hannah was immediately contrite but her anger would not lessen.

"Thank you, Miriam. I will be in contact with Isaac shortly." Her sister immediately retreated from the bedroom, closing the door in her wake but Hannah heard her sister's stifled sob before she retreated down the stairs. Hannah knew that her tone had been unreasonably harsh but she could not seem to alleviate the insurmountable rage which had filled her since the horrendous accident her father had endured a mere month before. The driver who had injured Mark so severely on that lone road heading home from the city had yet to be caught and Hannah knew she would not rest until the person had been apprehended and brought to justice. Christmas had come and gone in an unmemorable blur, still filled with family and friends but in a much more somber tone than the joy of the season typically brought. The family had left the candles lit in the windows well after other members of the community had extinguished theirs, a constant flame for others to keep Mark in their prayers. Hannah remembered thinking that the nativity scene was ruined and she had reprimanded Rachel harshly for playing with the wooden characters, reducing the child to a blubbering mess. Much more than that, Hannah could not recall about holiday. There had been an exchange of gifts but Mark's had lay unopened at the hearth and Hannah did not have any recollection of what she had received. Hannah's mother had continued her duty, tending to the farm and caring for the children and Hannah had stepped in to assist as opposed to joining Isaac. At first, Isaac had attempted to stay nearby, offering his unselfish aide to the Yoder family but eventually Hannah's increasingly sullen behavior had driven him home to his family's land. Still, he had frequently visited his beloved to see how she was faring. More often than not, Hannah made herself unavailable for reasons no one could comprehend. While she never admitted it to anyone, she blamed Isaac also for her father's fate. *If only he had been more vigilante, heeded my words more carefully when I suggested that something was amiss with father,* she told herself time and again. It did not matter that Mark Yoder had been hit on the Saturday night, well before Hannah had any inkling that there was trouble. In Hannah's grief she was beyond reason and all she had remaining was her intense anger. It was irrelevant whom was the recipient of her rage. It needed to be released and Hannah ensured that it was so. Mark's initial prognosis had been grim. The internal damage to his organs was severe and he had several broken bones. He was still on a life support machine in the hospital where he had been taken following being struck. Hannah could not bear to see her strong, vital father in such a condition and had refused to attend his side despite her mother's pleading.

"Hannah, your father needs you there," Ruth had begged her daughter. "Please swallow your repulsion and spend some time at his side. He can hear your prayers."

"He can hear my prayers from here, Mamm. It makes not difference if I am here or there. I cannot bear to see him in such a state with wires poking out of him. Hospitals are filled with harsh lights and harsher people," Hannah countered. "I will not be any good to him there. He knows I am with him in spirit."

Any amount of argument had been futile and eventually Ruth gave up, attending the county hospital with only her two youngest.

"God will not allow him to be taken from us," Ruth assured Hannah one night, attempting to connect with her distraught oldest child.

"God should not have allowed him to have been struck in the first place!" Hannah had yelled back. "God should have been watching out for him. God should have rendered the driver comatose and on life support!"

There was no point in debating the issue. In her mind, Hannah would not rest until she saw the face of the person responsible for the atrocity writhing in shame, guilt and agony.

<u>February</u>

"Ma'am I understand your anger but there we are doing everything we can."

Hannah's blue eyes flashed but she checked her temper.

"Sir, it has been almost three months and you have absolutely no leads regarding the driver of the vehicle which struck my father. Surely you should be exploring other avenues to catch this animal! Doesn't it concern you that this kind of person is driving on your streets where your children walk?"

"Hannah!" Isaac gently placed his hand on her shoulder as she rose from her chair to confront the police detective at the desk. He turned apologetically to the detective.

"Hannah has been under a lot of stress since the accident," Isaac told the man who nodded understandingly.

"Of course, we fully get that and we sympathize," Detective Adams replied. "I have heard that your father is no longer on life support. We are all very happy to hear that."

Hannah felt her hands clench into fists, her nails digging into her palms.

"Yes, praise the Lord for small favors," she answered shortly, her eyes narrowing, ignoring Isaac's fingers which were now increasing pressure on her shoulder. "However, that does not change anything. Is this why nothing has been done to find the monster responsible? Because he is alive? Next time he may not be so lucky if this person is still on the road!"

"Miss Yoder, I assure you that we are doing everything we can but it is very difficult with the circumstances. There were no witnesses, it was a dark road..."

Hannah threw up her hands. She understood. Mark Yoder was not a priority to these people. He would have to be dead or English for them to care. They were just going to say words until she left them alone. Worried she would not be able to contain a barrage of words threatening to escape her lips, she turned to leave without responding. Hannah heard Isaac apologizing for her rudeness once more but Hannah did not wait for her fiancé. Moments later, he was at her side, breathing heavily from chasing her down the crowded street. Under normal circumstances, Hannah would have been unnerved by the throng of people in her midst. It was not like her to visit town, much preferring the quiet way of her community but it had been months and there had been no advancement regarding the driver who had struck her father. Against her mother's pleas, Hannah had taken it upon herself to meet with the detective face-to-face.

"Please, Hannah, Bishop Phillips has been in constant contact with the police. You must not go and bother them."

"If not me, then who?" Hannah had demanded.

"Go see your father! He needs you!" Ruth implored. But the words had fallen upon deaf ears and Ruth had summoned Isaac to accompany her now wayward daughter into town. Isaac had appeared as Hannah was setting off.

"Hannah! That was rude!" He breathed, struggling to keep up with her brisk stride.

"Well perhaps that's what they need, rudeness. Niceties don't seem to be getting us anywhere."

"Hannah, I'm sure they are doing everything they can – "

"It is not enough!" Hannah snapped. Isaac stopped walking, taken aback by her tone. Hannah had never had occasion to speak to him in such a manner. He watched after the woman he was destined to marry and he wondered what had happened to the gentle, even tempered girl he had courted. He understood she was frazzled, not acting rationally but deep down, he hoped that girl was not lost forever.

<u>March</u>

"Hannah, you have not been at worship in several weeks."

The statement was blunt but not filled with accusation. Bishop Phillips simply stared at her, his brown eyes wise with understanding. She shrugged nonchalantly and did not turn from the hens from which she was collecting eggs.

"God knows where I am," she responded flippantly. Bishop Phillips drew closer to her inside the coop, ignoring the squawking of the animals in his midst.

"It is not simply of God knowing where to find you," he told her, gently. "Worship is a place of community, a place where others can shoulder your burden while asking for the Lord's help."

Hannah reeled around to glare at him.

"What does the community know of shouldering my burden?" she asked. "Can they find the animal who ran down my father like a rabid dog in the street? Have they made him pay penance for the harm he has caused my family?"

A warm, fatherly hand reached her shoulder and the Bishop smiled weakly.

"Perhaps not, child, but your suffering is our suffering also. We grow together and we will support one another. That is what makes us strong. You cannot fight this burden alone."

"I am not alone," Hannah retorted. "I have my family. I have Isaac."

But even as she said the words, Hannah tried to remember the last time she had spent more than a few moments with her betrothed. She could not. She shoved the thought from her mind. It did not matter. The only importance was figuring out who had hurt her father. Isaac would have to understand that her priority was with her father.

April

"Hannah! Hannah!"

Miriam and Rachel's footsteps could be heard reverberating through her bedroom well before the door flew open and the twins appeared. Her heart in her throat, Hannah turned away from the window out of which she had been staring for well over an hour, lost in thought.

"What is it? Is it *Daed*? Is he dead?"

Shocked, the girls recoiled at her words, smiles fading from their lips.

"No!" Rachel cried. "Of course not! Why would you say such a thing?"

In truth, Hannah had been waiting for news of the like and had been since the day he had been hospitalized. Her heart began to slow and she forced herself to smile at her sisters.

"I'm sorry. What is it?"

"He's awake! *Daed* is awake!"

Hannah's slowing pulse picked up speed once more. She flung herself into her siblings' arms and the three rejoiced at the news.

"He is? When did this happen? What did the doctors say?" Hannah whipped the questions at them rapid fire. Ruth appeared in the doorway. Her face was gaunt from exhaustion and emotion.

"He will still need some time to recover in the hospital," Ruth answered. "But his ribs are healing as well as his kidneys." Hannah pulled away from the twins and looked at her mother, her face alight with excitement. *Now we will catch you! Daed will identify the driver and it will all be over!*

"Did he say anything?" she pressed. "Can he identify the driver? Or the vehicle? Does he know who hit him?"

Ruth's sky colored eyes clouded over and she regarded her daughter for a moment.

"Hannah, it is not healthy for you to focus so direly on the driver. God will sort out what to do with him. You must instead think of your father and concentrate on good thoughts." Hannah scowled at her mother.

"I am focussed on *Daed*! That is why I want to find out who did this to him! Why am I met with resistance at every turn? You, Isaac, Bishop Phillips. Am I the only one who cares about seeing justice served?"

Ruth pursed her lips together and did not reply. Hannah continued to stare at her mother.

"Well? What did he say? Did he identify the man or not?" she demanded. Ruth sighed heavily.

"No, Hannah. He cannot speak. He had a stroke."

May

Springtime held the promise of new birth for everyone in the community but Hannah. She found herself tending to chores indoor more and more. Isaac had ceased visiting altogether and Hannah found herself in the police station once a week, hounding Detective Adams mercilessly. Where the women in the community would have typically begun to make suggestions for her wedding, offering assistance and chattering cheerfully of their own nuptials, Hannah found herself almost isolated, something she was quite content in discovering. The feeling of helplessness which had overwhelmed her was becoming a suffocating blanket as more time passed and left her no closer to finding the heathen who had hurt her father. She still had not gone to the hospital to see Mark, despite reports from her family that he was faring quite well. He still had not managed to recoup his motor skills and Hannah did not want the face of a crippled man plaguing her already dark thoughts. She would not rest until someone had paid.

June

"You are attending service."

Her voice was flat and left no room for argument. Hannah opened her mouth to speak but caught the anger in her mother's usually gentle eyes and thought better of voicing her thoughts. Grudgingly, she retreated to her room to ready herself for worship.

The family hosting church services was a neighbor and the Yoder family arrived just as Bishop Phillips rose to speak. He fixated his eyes upon Hannah and began to preach of forgiveness. Hannah closed her ears and averted her eyes. *I will forgive when the driver asks for forgiveness. Not one moment before. And even then, I may not.*

July

He came home on a Tuesday and several members of the community were present to welcome Mark. They brought flowers and honey and bombarded him and the family with well wishes. Isaac and his family had driven in also but Hannah only watched the event from her bedroom window, unable to watch her enfeebled father slowly stumble his way up the steps of the veranda. Her eyes filled with tears but whether they were of guilt or pain, she was not sure. As Mark made his way inside with the help of his wife and two youngest daughters, Isaac lifted his eyes toward Hannah's bedroom window. His own eyes were filled with sadness and Hannah quickly ducked back behind the curtains, not willing to look at him. It had been a long while since they had spent time together and she admitted that she missed his company dearly. She often wondered what he was doing and if he thought of her. The look on his face told Hannah that he did long for her as she did him. Swallowing the urge to run downstairs and beg him for forgiveness, Hannah sat on the edge of the bed. She wondered if anything would ever be the same again.

August

"Hannah! Hannah!"

Rachel almost knocked Hannah over as she barreled into the barn. Hannah looked up at her quickly.

"What is it?"

"*Daed* said his first clear word!" Hannah felt hope swell in her chest.

"What did he say?" she asked, wiping her hands on her apron and following Rachel out of the building, toward the house.

"He said 'Hannah.' He's asking for you!"

September

Progress was swift from that moment onward. Every day, Mark Yoder began to say more. He was required to see a specialist in town to assist him in his walking but Hannah was beginning to see signs of the same, strapping man she had admired her whole life. She found it less painful to be in his presence but she still could not help but feel enraged at his condition. When Hannah did stay at his side, she pressed him for details of the accident. To her relief, he recalled a great deal and Hannah feverishly wrote down the details as Mark remembered, every day adding more to the description. Finally, after three weeks, she had a proper sketch of the vehicle and possibly the driver which she immediately took to the police station. *Now we've got you!* She thought smugly.

October

"Are we still to marry?"

The question startled Hannah as she had not heard Isaac at her back. He had been watching her from the porch as she hummed to herself, picking wildflowers. Oddly, the upcoming wedding had been fresh in her mind for the first time in months. Since delivering the description to the police, Hannah had felt as though they were nearing absolution and a giant weight seemed to have been lifted from her shoulders. She stared in surprise at her fiancé.

"I certainly hope so, Isaac. Are you reconsidering?" She felt faint as she waited for him to answer. Slowly, Isaac made his way down the steps and toward his betrothed.

"I feel as though we have become very distant these past months, Hannah. I wondered if you still wished for us to marry." She met the distance between them and offered him her hands.

"Forgive me, Isaac! I have been consumed with worry for my father. Of course I have never thought for a moment that you and I would not be wed." Isaac eagerly accepted her hands and squeezed them gently, smiling with relief.

"I am glad you have finally decided to forgive and move on," he told her. "I knew the sensible woman I know was in there somewhere."

Hannah beamed back at him.

"It will be very easy to move on once this man is caught! I believe the police will finally catch him now!"

The smile died on Isaac's lips as he stared at Hannah. He realized that she was still consumed with the idea of catching the driver. Wisely, he said nothing but a sense of unease filled his stomach. Would this never end?

<u>November</u>

"You must be very excited with the upcoming wedding, Hannah. It has been quite a year for you and your family. It will be a relief to have cause for celebration over bad times, I would say," Bishop Phillips said after service. Hannah smiled widely and nodded, glancing at Isaac. He smiled meekly.

"Yes, we are looking forward to it. A Christmas wedding may seem a bit ostentatious but it is my favorite time of year and Isaac has been kind enough to indulge my whimsy on this matter," Hannah answered happily.

"Well I think it is a wonderful idea. It will only solidify your union with Christ. I am happy to see your father up and about."

"Yes, he is already back into manning the farm as he was prior to the accident."

"Well that is wonderful news, Hannah. It must certainly alleviate your desire to see the perpetrator arrested. It was not good for you to be so fixated on such negative thoughts for so long," the Bishop told her, turning to nod at other members of the congregation.

"No, Bishop, I can focus on other things now. The police are closing in on the animal now that my father has given them somewhere to look. We will have our justice in due time. I must leave it in their hands now." The Bishop looked at Hannah sharply.

"Your father knows who hit him?"

"He gave a very accurate description of the man, yes," Hannah replied. "But as you say, Bishop, it is in God's hands now. I have decided to focus more on my husband-to-be and deal with the criminal when he is found."

Bishop Phillips nodded, his eyes dark.

"Yes, it is in God's hands," he agreed.

December

The police were standing on her porch and Hannah felt her heart leap into her throat.

"Miss Yoder? Is your father home?" the detective asked her, peering over her shoulder. She nodded eagerly and granted them entry. Mark sat in a rocking chair in the front room. He rose to his feet with an agility he did not possess even two weeks prior.

"Please do come in, officers," he told them, cordially. Awkwardly, the detectives ventured into the humble home and stood in the doorway.

"Have you found the man responsible?" Hannah demanded. "Is that why you're here?"

Mark gave her a reproachful look.

"Hannah, where are your manners? Would you like a beverage?" Both men shook their heads and fidgeted nervously.

"Well?" Hannah demanded when there was silence. "Have you news?"

"Hannah!" Mark chided again but the lead detective held up his hand and nodded.

"Yes, Miss Yoder. We have your man. Someone has turned himself in."

Hannah's face went through a variety of changes; hope, shock and then anger.

"He turned himself in?" she almost yelled. "After one year? What kind of monster lets a family suffer for an entire year before confessing his crime?"

"Hannah..."

"Yes, Miss Yoder but frankly, in these situations, it is extremely difficult to find hit and run drivers. We are very lucky that someone did come forward at all," the policeman interjected. "But I do understand your frustration."

"I doubt it," Hannah mumbled. "Where is he?"

"He is in the county lock up. We would like your father to come with us to see if he can be identified in a line up but he had fully confessed to the accident."

"Who is he? A young, drunk English boy?" Hannah asked contemptuously, already envisioning the short haired punk, smoking a marijuana cigarette. Again, an uncomfortable silence ensued. Hannah stared at the men expectantly.

"Who is he?"

Detective Adams cleared his throat.

"It is someone you know," he said evasively. Hannah exchanged concerned looks with her father.

"Who?" she pressed.

"He is your Bishop. Daniel Phillips."

"Hello Hannah."

Hannah felt her legs turn to jelly as she stared at her much-loved Bishop behind the bars of the county jail.

"It is true," she whispered. "How did this happen?"

"I wish I could explain it to you, child but there is nothing I can say which will take away what you and your family have endured over this year."

"Please tell me what happened," she begged, her eyes filled with tears. The Bishop took a breath and told her the story he had relived in his head over and over since the day it had happened.

He had travelled the road hundreds, if not thousands of times before but Bishop Phillips had not slept more than two hours a night in over three weeks. There had been minor unrest in two of the neighboring districts, some petty squabbling which should have resolved itself but somehow a miniscule issue had become a weeks long debate. He was grateful that he was finally able to return home to his district. The car in which he rode had been a gift from a Bishop in one of the districts who had taken pity upon his constant state of commute. Bishop Phillips had to admit that it was more luxurious than his hard riding horse and cart but he also knew that he should not get too attached.

As the headlights lit the way around the road, his heart leapt into his throat. A doe stood frozen in the road, shocked by the onset. In his exhaustion, it took a few seconds for his reaction time to match up with his vision. He slammed on the brakes and veered to the left of the road, barely grazing the tail of the animal but full on impacting something else; a horse drawn cart. The mare whinnied in pain and shock as the Bishop struggled to steady the still moving vehicle. As all was still, Bishop Phillips opened the door to the car and ran toward the now toppled buggy. Inside lay the still body of Mark Yoder, seemingly lifeless. Bishop Phillips stood stock still, unsure of what to do. I must stay and wait for help, he told himself. Then he remembered the two glasses of wine he had consumed with supper. Slowly, he backed up and slipped back into the car, driving away undetected into the black night.

Tears fell from her lids onto her cheeks as she looked at the broken man before her. She thought of how badly she had wanted him to suffer but all she could think of was how much he had already suffered. He must have wanted to ease her agony a thousand times but had been trapped in his own nightmare.

"I understand that you must loathe me, Hannah. You have every right to feel as such," Bishop Phillips told her, his voice cracking. Gently, Hannah reached between the bars and offered the Bishop her hands. He grabbed them instantly and looked at her pleadingly.

"I forgive you," she said simply.

<u>Christmas</u>

"Oh, Hannah you look beautiful," Ruth told her daughter, embracing her warmly. "I have been looking forward to this for so long!"

Hannah laughed.

"Yes, me too Mammi," she joked and lovingly returned her mother's caress. She looked at herself in the mirror one last time. She vowed to her reflection that with this new start she would forsake all anger and rely on God to give her strength in the worst of times. She knew how fortunate she was that Isaac had been strong enough to stand by her during such a trying time and she would never forget it. She turned and looked at her mother and sisters.

"Are you ready?" Miriam asked, hopping back and forth from one foot to another. Hannah looked around and suddenly her stomach dropped.

"Where is *Daed*?" she asked, feeling a familiar sense of panic seize her. The curtain was quickly drawn and Mark strolled in, his gait strong and perfect.

"I am here, *liebchen*. Do you think I would miss giving away my oldest daughter?" he answered. His voice was slightly slower than it had been but his words were perfectly pronounced. There was no sign of the stroke he had suffered. Hannah exhaled. Everything was right again.

TO TRUST AGAIN

65

NATASHA GROVER

To trust again...

When Annie's long-time boyfriend decides that the Amish way was no longer his way, she is left shattered, but worst of all single. She struggles to overcome rejection and prays for God to help her, but all she gets in return is silence. Barren and a spinster, she had lost all hope of finding love. But through revelation during a Sunday service, she discovers that there is hope, and that is when everything changes.

When Seth and his daughter Mary arrive in town, everything changes. A chance meeting with a beautiful woman who adores his daughter was nothing but the grand design of God.

God works in mysterious ways, and this is exactly what happens when two souls are meant for each other.

Chapter 1

Annie looked down at the small keepsake box Abel gave her last Christmas. She never thought she would feel this way, so deserted and lost. Abel was the only man she ever cared for and now he was gone, out of her life and out of her world, but still so very present in her mind. She couldn't believe it when he came to her just a month ago to tell her he was leaving for good. Everything seemed so perfect, she was happy; she thought he was happy and although he often told her how he would have liked to be able to study science instead of erecting barns and toil in the fields, she never expected him to follow that farfetched dream of his. After all, his father was the Bishop of Lititz and he knew the consequences of his actions, yet here she was staring eternity in its face with no hope to marry one day. *How could God have allowed this to happen*, she thought as tears welled up in her eyes, surely He would not have allowed such a worldly passion to overcome Abel and allow his servant and son to run into a world where evil is so rife.

"Annie, it's time to let it go," Anke said as she came to stand next to her.

"Not now Anke," Annie mumbled, wiping the tears from her cheeks.

"You've been a walking corpse since he left, you hardly eat and all you do is sit here and sulk, sooner or later the pain will go away, but only if you let it go."

"It's easy for you to say, you have everything," she blurted out and stormed into the house to find the solitude of her room.

Anke was her younger sister, what did she know of heartbreak? It wasn't as if she could simply turn off a switch and stop feeling so terrible. She was married, she had everything Annie ever wanted, she had a loving husband a child and her life was perfect. Anke knew better than to envy her sister, but her emotions were all over the place and right now not in the best of places either. If only she could turn back time and try harder to convince Abel to stay. But now that she had time to think things over it became more and more evident why Abel never proposed to marry her. He never intended to stay, and after Bishop King's passing, there was nothing to stop him from pursuing his dream. If he loved her like he so often said, then why did he break her heart? He didn't even ask her to join him, not that she would have, but if he had asked her then she would have been certain that he did in fact see a future with her, but then it would have been her choice to stay. But instead he went on his own, because he wanted to leave everything behind, including her.

She slammed the door to her room shut and pressed her back up against it, this raging sea of anger was suffocating her in ways unimaginable. She was angry with Abel, with Anke and even with her youngest sister Mabel. Convicted by the thought of being angry even with God, she tossed the keepsake box aside and fell to her knees.

"Forgive me Father; I'm a simple person with a broken heart. Please take away this pain and heartache," she prayed as tears streamed down her face, "Please help me to understand why everything is going wrong in my life. Have I not been a loyal servant?"

She waited expectantly for an answer or for the pain to miraculously disappear, but the silence was like a poison that seeped into her blood and paralyzed her. The emptiness she felt was overwhelming and cruel, "Why have Thou forsaken me?" she cried. It felt as if God had turned his back on her, even though she had no idea why. She searched the recesses of her mind, trying to make sense of it all, trying to remember any sins she may not have asked forgiveness for, but nothing came to mind. Rejected by her one true love and by God, she curled up on the floor and wept.

Chapter 2

Two days have passed, since her melt down in front of her sister, and thankfully Anke did not poke at her again, but the emptiness was far from gone. Numb she sat against the wall in Bishop Troyer's house with everyone else occupying the space for the Sunday Service. She felt almost alienated and the looks of sympathy she got from her peers didn't help her mood either, she was an utter disgrace, not to mention humiliating. All the other women her age was settled down with their own families. And at the age of twenty-nine she had nothing but broken dreams strewn in the wake of a failed relationship.

Caught up in her own thoughts she paid little attention to the service, until Bishop Troyer clapped his hands together and exclaimed loud enough for her to pay attention, "Trust in the Lord with all your heart and lean not on your own understanding; in all your ways submit to him, and he will make your paths straight."

That was her moment of realisation, all this time she had been trying to make sense of it all with her own understanding. And she was too emotional to thing rational, she still had a lot of questions as to why God had taken Abel from her when she was so sure they were promised to one day marry, but if she was going to get through all of this she was going to have to put her trust in God.

After the service she felt less burdened, almost as if a weight had been lifted, the longing was still there but it was lighter than before and instead of going home she took a walk down the small path that led to the a nearby brook. A time for reflection was nigh and by the grace of the Father, she could finally be free. She sat down in grass near the stream and closed her eyes, raising her face to the sun and soaking in it warmth. The spinning chaos that had altered her world over the past month or so was suddenly replaced by hope and for that she was grateful for.

"Daed!" a little voice called not far from where Annie was sitting and she quickly opened her eyes and looked up stream, and then she saw the little girl in her blue dress skipping towards her, and not far behind her, her father or so she would assume.

"Hello," the little girl said as she reached her, "why are you sitting here?"

"Mary, where are your manners?" her father reprimanded when he reached her, "I'm so sorry, she gets out of hand quite quickly," he apologised and Annie simply smiled.

"It's quite alright, I was just enjoying the fresh air," she said to the little girl, "My name is Annie," she smiled and extended her hand to the little girl, who suddenly shyly hid behind her father.

"She's embarrassed now," he chuckled and pulled her out from behind his legs, "Say hello to Annie."

"Hello Annie," the little girl, who couldn't have been older than five or six years greeted, with her thumb stuck in her mouth and her toes pointed to each other.

Annie did not recognize them, although their community was sizable and she didn't know a few people by name, she would surely have remembered the faces. And as far as she can recall she hadn't seen the little girl at the local school where she often helps out as a teacher's aid, but then she may not be six yet.

"I'm Seth," he said and tipped his hat, "Mary likes to come here whenever we come to Lititz."

So they were not from around here, she realized raising her hand to cover the bright sunlight streaming down from above, "Where are you from?"

"Rothsville, we came to attend the church service at least once a year in honour of my belated wife."

Annie's heart cramped in her chest, as she realized he was widowed, yet his tone of voice sounded uplifting as if he had made peace with his loss.

"Mamm died of cancer," little Mary piped up.

She had a maturity level Annie hadn't seen in a child for a long time, and realized that it may be because of her loss.

"My condolences to you," she cleared her throat, "It must be a difficult time for you."

"It's been a year and some months now, Meryl was from here originally, and I promised her that I will bring Mary here, she always liked it here by the stream."

"Why do you come here?" Mary asked again and this time Annie pushed herself up to on to her feet.

"Well I like the stream too, especially the flowers that grow on the banks," she smiled and ironed down the front of her dress, "But I'm done now, so you can play here as long as you want."

"Oh no, you don't have to leave," Seth objected.

Annie smiled at him and shook her head, "I have to get going anyway, and I only came here for a little while to clear my head."

"Why don't you stay?" Mary pleaded and tugged on her hand.

Annie's heart warmed to the little girl, she was adorable. With big blue eyes and blonde curly hair that stuck out from under her bonnet. She was sure that Mary was Seth's ray of sunshine.

"Maybe next time, I have to go and prepare food with my sisters."

"Let go of Annie's hand Mary," Seth instructed his daughter and pried her away, "I'm sure we will meet each other again and then you can invite Mary to join you here at the stream."

"What a lovely idea," she smiled, "maybe I will pack a few eats for the next time you come here."

Little Mary nodded excitedly and Seth simply smiled at her, which caused her tummy to tumble. He was a handsome man, and probably not much older than her. Not to mention his lovely little girl.

"I will see you around some time," Annie said and then waved as she headed up the small path.

What a chance meeting, she thought. Here she was down and out and God had just revealed to her that He is still in control, and then she meets this charming little family, who despite their loss, can still smile and radiate such hope and passion that it could ignite a fire. Just to see them together warmed her heart. She looked back again and smiled as little Mary waved back at her.

Chapter 3

Seth looked at Mary where she played on the edge of the stream, floating leaves like little boats downstream. Every now and again she placed a pebble on one of the bigger leaves and when it didn't sink she squealed excitedly. She reminded him so much of Meryl, her summer blonde hair that curled like her mothers' and the dimples that indented on her cheeks when she smiled. It's been over a year since his wife had passed away from cancer, and although he accepted it a long time ago, he's only now starting to feel human again now. He had been on autopilot since her death, having had to focus on Mary and raising her, in a way he was grateful that he had his little girl. Having someone to depend on him during such a difficult time eased the hurt and pain somewhat. That was the way of life, the weak always cares for the weak, it is how God intended it. He just wishes he could have been able to save Meryl, then she could still be here watching Mary grow up.

He lay back in the grass, hitched up on one arm, He dared not question God, he knew that through the storm, God had a plan and he was going to wait on God to reveal that plan no matter how long it takes.

His thoughts shifted to the woman he had met earlier, she wasn't young enough to be unwed, and she wasn't a widow, but yet she is unattached, which he found strange. A woman with such a beautiful smile would have many possible suitors.

"Seth!" a distant voice drew him out of his reverie.

He looked up and noticed William headed his way. William was one of his friends who lived here, and whenever he came to visit, he stayed with him. He raised his hand and waved, still keeping a vigilant eye on Mary.

"Finding you is no easy task," William said as he reached him.

"You know I bring Mary here right after church whenever I'm in town," Seth said and chuckled as Mary jumped up and down to cheer on her fleet of leaves.

"She's grown up since I last saw her."

"Yes she has, but we haven't been here for some time."

"True," William nodded, "I actually came to ask if you would be up to help us out with a barn rising. Our planner, well he upped and left unexpectedly and we need someone with skill to draw up the plans."

A barn raising, it's been years since Seth had taken part in any of those, the last time he did was over three years prior to his wife's passing. He had to admit, the thought of staying here while longer was tempting. Mary will get to come here every day, he would be able to put his skills to the test, and maybe, just maybe he will be able to get to meet Annie again. That thought crept in there without warning and he quickly cleared his throat and mentally shook his head. There was no time in his life for romance; he had a daughter to care for and a business to run. As a carpenter he prided himself in the work he could do, simple yet sophisticated pieces of furniture, sold not only to the Amish community but also to outsiders who valued solid oak furniture. And with the off cuts he made small ornaments and bird houses which he sold at a local stand just outside Rothsville.

"So what happened to the other chap?" he asked curiously.

"He got tired of our ways and headed out into the world."

"That's a pity, but I guess I can hang around a little longer if you don't mind that Mary and I stay on at your place."

"Of course I won't mind, you're always welcome here you know that."

The sudden jolt of excitement made Seth grin from ear to ear. It looks like this year was a year of the Lord's favour; he will finally get to work on something significant again.

He called for Mary and she quickly came skipping towards him, she was going to be so happy to stay here, he just knew it.

"How would you like to stay here for a few weeks?" he said as he knelt down on one knee, while dusting off dry leaves and grass from her dress.

Her infectious smile spread across her face and her eyes lit up, "Really *Daed*?" she said with her child like enthusiasm, "Will I get to see Annie?"

Taken by surprise that she actually mentioned Annie, he cast a quick glance to William, who stood with his arms crossed and an amused expression on his face.

"She was here at the brook when we got here, Annie likes her," he fibbed for an excuse.

"Sure she does," William smirked.

"Can I daed, can I?" she pleaded as she hopped unto his one knee.

"I'm sure we can make a plan," he said, how could anyone say no to such a face.

As the three of them headed back up the small hill towards civilization, Seth couldn't help but think about Annie, the friendly yet mysterious woman with the radiating smile, who seemed to have captured his daughter's attention. She had never taken to any other woman like this before, not even Grace, Meryl's younger sister.

"A penny for your thoughts," William said and grinned at him.

Seth chuckled and hooked his thumbs into his suspenders, he might as well be out with it, "It's been more than a year since Meryl passed away, sooner or later Mary will need a woman to teach her how to conduct herself appropriately. Teach her how to quilt and bake bread and so on."

"And you're thinking of Annie?" Willian asked as he kicked a stone out of the way.

"Not specifically, but meeting her and seeing how much Mary enjoyed her company made me think about it."

Who was he kidding, of course he was thinking of Annie. He met some other women from his own town who were all too willing to step up and fill Meryl's shoes but he never really paid any attention to their advances. But now out of the blue, all he could seem to think of was her.

She was heaven sent, no doubt and if he didn't at least try, he would never know.

"Ay, well, Annie has had her heart broken and she's been a difficult one to get on with ever since, so good luck."

"Did it happen recently?" he asked curiously.

"About a month ago, you know the planner I told you about? Abel was his name. He just came out one day, said his good byes and left. I believe he went to New York to study science."

"And left her behind too..."

Seth felt a great deal of sympathy for her, and his heart ached. He could only imagine how much pain she must have gone through when that happened. It's one thing to send someone off to the beyond, but having someone leave out of free will to explore the world out there was like a slap in the face.

"Yeah, it was rather sad, they looked happy together."

"Clearly he was not happy, otherwise he would not have broken her heart," Seth defended.

He knew that he was going to have to take one step at a time with Annie, and not push her into anything she didn't want. But if there was one thing he would do for her, whether they ended up together or not, was to show her that God has a plan for all his children.

Chapter 4

The quietness of the early morning was peaceful, there were no birds singing their morning songs or a rooster crowing to announce the start of a new day and the sun was still buried behind the horizon. Annie closed her eyes again as the heady pull of her dreams beckoned her back to play, but she had to wake up. There was too much to do on this blessed day. The past month she spent wallowing in self-pity had robbed her of some precious time such as baking bread and taking it to the local store, not to mention her chocolate cookies everyone always used to love so much. And maybe if she was lucky, she may be able to get some of those cookies to Mary before she departed with her father.

Even for an overcast day, nothing could dispel the mood Annie was in, for the first time in weeks, she felt alive again and ready to take on the world.

"You're up early," Eva said as she entered the kitchen, "and you're baking?"

Annie smiled at her youngest sister and nodded, "Yes, it's time I stop fussing over Abel and get on with life."

Eva ran around the table and threw her arms around her neck, "Thank goodness! We were all getting so worried about you. I'm so glad you've come to your senses."

Annie laughed and hugged her sister back, it's only now that she realized just how much she inconvenienced everyone around her and she was relieved that it had all come to an end. Yes, she may still think of Abel from time to time, but it no longer affected her as it did just a day ago before God had spoken to her heart. And if she can embrace the change with a positive attitude, then she will only be blessed richly.

"I'm sorry I had you all so worried, but it's all in the past now," she said as tears sprung to her eyes.

"No need to apologize, you and Abel were together for a very long time."

Eva released her and reached for one of the cookies on the cooling rack, and then picked up her quilt basket, "I have to go, but when I get back I want to hear how on earth this paradigm shift took place."

"Of course," Annie laughed and swatted her sister's hand away, "These are for Mary, and I'll bake another batch for the house later this afternoon."

"Who's Mary? Oh wait, don't tell me, I'm going to be late, but when I get back later you can tell me everything."

And like a whirlwind Eva left the house.

Later than morning after delivering the baked flat breads to the local store Annie's mood had taken a turn for the worst, but not because of Abel. She had hoped to see Mary and Seth but it seemed that she was too later. The realization that they had left to go back to Rothsville left her empty. She should have asked them when they were leaving instead of putting in all the effort to bake cookies for Mary. A soft sigh escaped her lips as she made her way towards Anke's house, at least the cookies will be put to good use there, she thought.

"Mary!" A little voice called out to her and Anke's heart leapt with joy and she spun around.

"There you are," she smiled, "I thought you had gone back home."

"Oh no, daed said that we'll be staying here while he builds a barn," she exclaimed and hugged Annie's leg.

"She beat me to it," Seth said when he reached them.

Annie's heart fluttered in her chest and she smiled up at him, next to him the top of her head only reached his shoulder. She was just as excited as the toddler clinging to her dress having learned that they will be staying on for a while. Normally Abel would be the one drawing up the plans for the barn and making sure everything was in order. It used to be so exciting watching him loose himself I the work.

"Where will you be staying?"

"We'll be staying with William and his wife; he was kind enough to open his door for us."

"That's good yah," and she went down on her knees to get to Mary's level, "I baked you some chocolate cookies," she said holding out the small tin.

Mary beamed and immediately took the tin from Annie and dug in.

"Thank you Annie," Seth said as she stood up, "Mary has really taken to you."

"She's a lovely child."

For a moment, Annie was lost in Seth's gaze and his smile that could make the world around her fade into the background. Mary had his smile with his dimples as well as his sky blue almond shaped eyes, there was no doubt that she was his daughter. The only difference was that he had he had brown hair. His wife must have been a beautiful woman, she thought briefly before little hands drew her attention again.

"Daed said that I can stay here today while he goes to fetch our clothes, only if I stay with you."

She was so caught up in her own thoughts she never heard that part of the conversation, and the toothy grin Mary gave her arrested her.

"Well, if you don't mind leaving her with a complete stranger, then I'm happy to take care of her for you," she smiled.

"You're not a complete stranger and William did say you were good with children."

So she had been a topic of discussion between him and William? Now more than ever, she was intrigued by Seth. But if she had been the topic of discussion hen surely William had divulged the bit of information about Abel.

"Of course!" she said out loud, "You're here to take over what Abel failed to complete," she blurted out unceremoniously.

"Pardon me?"

"Abel, he used to do the plans for the barns,"

"Oh yes, Abel. That's right. William asked me to help out."

A small frown creased on his forehead and Annie almost kicked herself, that wasn't even the conversation topic. The whole thing was about her taking care of Mary.

"I'll watch Mary for you," she railed back on to the topic, "we're going to have a lot of fun."

"Will you make my hair like yours?" Mary asked and Seth laughed.

"Like mine? But what is wrong with your hair, it looks beautiful."

"It's too curly and dead can never brush it."

She looked back at Seth and he shrugged, "It's always tangled, you have no idea how difficult it is to brush her hair."

"Well I have just the solution for your problem," Annie said grinning.

The poor father had no idea how to raise a daughter, and if she could help in any way she was more than happy to.

Chapter 5

Barn raising day...

It was a fine summer's day, and the weather couldn't be more perfect. The entire community had gathered to do the barn rising for the Yoder family, who had lost their barn in a fire two months ago, and while the women were all busy making food and helping with odds and ends, the men got ready for a hard day of teamwork.

Seth stood at the table at the far side of the grounds looking over his plans again. Although raising a barn was a much bigger project that putting together tables and chairs he was confident that I was flawless.

"So word has it that you're keen on Anny," William said as he came to stand beside him.

"Is that so?" Seth chuckled.

"Yah, yah, I've heard the talk in the town. Her sister Anke actually asked me outright if I knew anything."

Seth crossed his arms over his chest and glanced towards the tables where the women were gathered. There among them all sat Annie with Mary in deep conversation. He had only been here for two weeks, and during this time he had grown fond of her. But there was always the question that poked at his conscience. Was he attracted to her simply because she got on so well with Mary, or was he attracted to her because she was, well, Annie.

"She's a pretty woman, and she's very good with children," Seth admitted, trying not to say too much.

"Come on Seth, it's more than that. She's good with children yah, but she will make a fine wife. You should go on and talk to her."

"I'm sure she does, but I don't know if she is over Abel at all."

That was a truth he could not deny. She had hardly spoken about Abel during their meets at the creek, but the way she reacted that morning when she realized that he had taken the work Abel was meant to do, indicated that he still affected her. And how would he compete with that?

"Trust me, according to Anke, her entire mood changed since the day you arrived, she just needed a shove in the right direction."

"Well at least I accomplished something," Seth joked and elbowed William, "We can jabber on about her later, right now we have a barn to finish. Are the men ready to start?"

William shook his head and chuckled, "They are all ready, but if God wills for you two to get together, you know that no power on earth or in heaven can prevent that, right?"

"Then we shall see what God has in store."

William was right about one thing, if God had his hand in this and the only reason he ended up in this community was to meet Annie, then he prayed that God's will would reign over his fleshly emotions that have been running rampant of late. If not, then he will finish this barn here today, and return to Rothsville a sane but proud father.

By the end of the day the structure stood high against the afterglow of the setting sun, and families were slowly making their way home. Seth was pleased by the work that was accomplished in one day and the fact that he was able to lay out the plans to such perfection made him proud to say the least. With only the Yoder's left along with the odd family friends, Seth made his way to where Mary was helping Annie pack away the excess food. For a moment he looked at the two of them and couldn't help but smile. Annie really did like Mary, and if he had to be honest with himself, he liked her too. She was a beautiful woman with a heart of gold and a soft spot for Mary.

Chapter 6

The barn had finally been completed, and Annie knew all too well that soon she would have to say her farewells to Seth and Mary, and that thought alone left a lump in her throat. She really liked them, especially Mary. Annie swallowed at the lump in her throat; she would never be able to have her own children, not since the unfortunately surgery when she was only twenty that left her barren. And having been able to spend these few weeks with Mary really left her wishing for a miracle.

"You should tell him how you feel," Eva said at the breakfast table.

"You mean Seth?" Annie said blushing slightly.

Eva laughed and reached for Annie's hand, "Everyone can see that you two like each other. He's a widow and you're a spinster, you're simply perfect for each other."

"I would never be so forward!" Annie exclaimed laughing, "If he feels the way everyone assume he feels, then he would have to do the ground work."

Eva raised a brow, "And if he doesn't because he is to shy?"

"Then so be it, but I am not going to embarrass myself, what if everyone is wrong about him?"

"Trust me, we're not wrong."

Eva was persistent, for one she was young and full of happily ever after dreams; secondly, she was a self-proclaimed match maker. But even if Eva was right, Annie simply refused to put herself in the firing line. It would be up to God to guide her way, not her own understanding. Her own understanding when it came to Abel didn't help one bit, so she was going to have to simply put her trust in God and hope for the best outcome.

A slight knock on the door drew the sisters' attention and Eva was the first to rush to open the door and a few seconds later, it was Seth and Mary standing in their kitchen.

"Why don't you two join us for breakfast," Eva invited.

"Oh no, we've already had breakfast," Seth said, never taking his eyes of Annie.

Eva's gaze moved from Seth to Annie and back to Seth, when she raised both brows and fought to hide a smile.

"Mary, come with me, I want to show you my room."

Relieved Annie let out breathless sigh and stood up.

"I suppose you would have to go back to your home now that the Barn is up?"

The way Seth stood shifting his weight from one foot to the other, with his head in his hand made her smile, he looked so nervous. If only he could hear the frantic beating of her own heart.

"Yah, I have to go back. I have a business to run which I have neglected while staying here," he said and looked around the kitchen.

"I'm sorry," Annie said and cleared her throat, "I'm confident that God will help you make up time for your generous act of kindness to help the Yoder's."

Without warning, Seth stepped forward and came around the table until he stood in front of her. Of course her heart stopped and the zooming bees in her stomach did not help her one bit.

"Thank you for helping out with Mary," he said with his eyes downcast.

"That was no problem at all; maybe when you come back, I can help again."

She meant it, every word. She would do anything to spend some more time with Mary and teach her how to bake and quilt. The way she felt now, she wished that this would never end. But what she wished for more was for Seth to tell her how he felt.

"I've actually been thinking," he started and Annie held her breath.

"Yes?"

"Well, you get on so well with Mary, and well, we get on well too..." he paused and shuffled closer, "I know I'm not going about this the right way, but I was thinking or rather wondering if you would like to come with us to Rothsville."

Annie's mouth fell open and she stared at him, "You mean move there?

Seth nodded and shrugged, "We've only known each other for a short while, but when Jacob saw Rachel for the first time, he wanted to marry her right away..."

It felt as if Annie's entire world was turned on its axis and spinning in the opposite direction, did Seth just ask her to marry her or was she misunderstanding the meaning behind his words?

"What exactly are you proposing?" she said in a trembling voice.

"Oh for heaven's sake! He's asking if you'll marry him!" Eva shouted from the passageway.

Just then Mary came running out flinging her arms around Annie's legs.

Seth shrugged and smiled, "In short, yes. I mean I will go the Bishop first to ask for his blessing, but I have grown very fond of you and so has Mary, and after the time we spent together, I've come to realize that God had brought us to this place."

Her eyes shot full of tears and Eva lifted Mary up in her arms, twirling around and cheering, while her and Seth simply looked at each other.

A simple yes was all it took and Annie's dreams had come true. She found love in the strangest of circumstances and when she least expected too. On top of that, she would get to teach Mary everything that is good.

~*~

Seth could hardly have believed it was it not for the fact that he pinched himself for the umpteenth time. But there she stood, in her wedding garments. As beautiful as the first day he saw her near the brook and she was finally going to be his. But he knew that it was only by the hand of God that he had finally found a woman who will be good to both him and his daughter. And that was Annie, beautiful sweet spinster, Annie.

THE SHY AMISH BRIDE

87

NATALIE MEYER

Three best friends, Betty, Amity and Rachel are practically inseparable. But when they land themselves in a stormy predicament on their way home on night a newcomer in town comes to their rescue. All three girls show an interest in the handsome stranger, but only one of them would walk away with the prize. What starts off as nothing but a playful bet between friends, ends up surprising them all.

Uri Guth came to Derby Creek to start afresh, the last thing he expected was to fall in love. But when he meets the shy red head who reminded him autumn, he pulled out all stops. He knew the moment he laid eyes on her that she was his match.

Chapter 1

Rain just kept falling, never ending without any intention to stop, large puddles had gathered on the muddy grounds around the big barn, and water gushed down the eroded embankment running alongside the road, causing the road to be completely flooded. But no amount of rain would prevent Amity, Betty and Rachel to do what they came here to do. Having been friends since childhood, the three women were inseparable. Neither of them were married or promised to anyone yet, and although they are well beyond the age most girls in their community starts to settle down to start a family, it never really bothered them.

Amity was strong willed and mouthy young woman, who voiced her opinion whenever she felt it mattered. Of course her father, Bishop Gunther didn't quite approve of her behaviour at times, but he did support her willingness to stand up for herself. Bishop Gunther on the other hand wasn't like most others in their faith; he was more lenient and accepting than most, always promoting change within reason. He insisted that households started using gas stoves instead of coal stoves. He had even arranged to buy a truck to help the community to cart goods to the local market in town. According to him, modern change to a bare minimum does not give the devil a foothold, it just shows the devil that they are capable of change without modern ways ruling their lives and changing who they are or distracting them from things that matter most.

Betty, much like Amity also had a strong personality, one she definitely got from her mother, but she also had a mischievous streak. When the elders instructed the children not to play in the rain, she was always the first to splash in muddy puddles. When they had their social events, she was the one who would pull pranks, like stuff a mouse in someone's pocket or stick a dish to a table cloth with workman's glue, causing a huge disaster when someone tries to pick it up. All innocent pranks at most, but that was how everyone knew her and more often than not, when she was younger her father would ground her for punishment, but she always found a way out of it.

And then there was Rachel, shy quiet Rachel. More like the runt of the litter, she was one of few words and always just tagged along because Amity and Betty insisted. Rachel only had a father; her mother died giving birth to her. Her father eventually married Elsa, a widow with two sons, who she never got on with. They were two brats and she ended up spending more time with her friends than her own family and over the years, the trio had become the best of friends

Betty giggled and Amity squirmed on the bale of hay, "I bet you David looks like that when he takes his shirt off," she said pointing to the male model in the fashion magazine.

Amity giggled, "It's scandalous! If your dad knew you had these, he'll shun us all," she said in jest.

Rachel, curious as ever, was sitting on the left, also peeking at the magazine, one of the few they kept hidden in the barn under one of the wooden floor slats. They always snuck to the barn to page through the magazines and weigh every other man in their town up against the likes of models that posed so shamelessly with nothing but pair of underpants on.

"Jah! Well he doesn't know now does he?" Betty said and paged through a few more pages.

Rachel would never admit it out rightly but she also felt a slight tingle of excitement when she looked at these magazines, they were not overly crude, but they showed more flesh than she had ever seen in her life. Maybe it was because of this, that they were all still single, she thought. Comparing the local boys to those men were like comparing apples with onions.

A sudden noise quickly alerted them and Betty shoved the magazine behind the bale of hay they were seated on. Both Amity and Betty grabbed their egg baskets, while Rachel stood around looking as guilty as ever.

"Betty, are you girls here?"

It was Betty's father who called, and Rachel's stomach lurched, if the Bishop had any idea what they were up to they will be in so much trouble.

"We're here *daed*!" Betty called and dusted the hay off of her dress, "We were caught in the rain, and was waiting for it to pass," she said as her Bishop Gunther appeared.

"I thought so, well I have come to get you girls home, the storm is a long way from being over," he said and handed each of them a rain coat, "Better we hurry, or the storm will catch up with us," he urged them as he let each one of the girls walk towards the barn door ahead of him.

The sky was dark and it wasn't just a summer shower, it was a downpour that looked more like a waterfall from heaven. Heavy drops struck the ground tunnelling into the earth. Up ahead stood the buggy, which didn't offer much or any shelter and Rachel wasn't so sure if they would make it to their respective homes in one piece. Betty was the first to step into the rain, followed by Amity. Bishop Gunther looked at her and nodded, and then in a huddled group the four of them ran towards the buggy, careful not to slip and fall.

Thankful that there was still some daylight to guide the way, the three girls clung to each other as Betty's father steered the buggy towards the house. Hardly able to see a few feet ahead of them and on a treacherous road that has been washed away in most places, Bishop Gunther was still able to make them feel at ease. He didn't even look worried, but then again, that was probably how a man of God should be, like Paul walking on water.

The buggy wheels rattled as they rode over rocks and muddy trenches formed by the mass of water running diagonally across the small road. And a trip that normally took less than fifteen minutes to travel, now seemed like an eternity. They were slowly making their way ahead through the stormy downpour, unbeknownst to Bishop Gunther, the road up ahead had turned into complete sludge and the moment the buggy reached it, the wheels simply slid into a deep trench on the side of the road, pulling the buggy, with the horse off and on to the side of the road. The girls screamed in panic as the buggy slowly leaned over to its side, threatening to topple over. Rachel was the first to clobber out and then helped the other two on to the road. Betty got out safely, but as Amity stumbled out of the buggy, she stepped in a hole and twisted her ankle.

"Ow!!" she cried out as she fell to the ground grabbing for her ankle.

"Amity!" Betty cried and ducked down to help her friend, "Where does it hurt?"

Bishop Gunther also hunched down and looked at her ankle, "It's quite swollen, I think you may have sprained it, can you try and step on it?"

Betty and her father helped Amity to her feet, but the moment she put weight on her injury, she cried out in agony.

"We will have to get you home, just lean on me and Betty" the Bishop said. He studied the state of the buggy, "The buggy will have to stay here until morning."

"But papa, we can hardly see in front of us," Betty lamented as she supported her friend.

"The Lord will light our way," Rachel said confidently and gave Betty a gentle reassuring squeeze.

With Amity supported by Bishop Gunther and Betty, and Rachel next to them carrying the egg baskets, they started down the path taking carful steps in the dark.

Through the stormy gale and rain that kept showering, they heard a galloping sound that sounded more like thunder coming towards them and the next moment, a man on horseback arrived completely drenched.

Rachel couldn't make out his face, but right now he was the best thing that could have happened to them.

"Bishop, Maryanne sent me to see what was keeping you," he shouted over the raging storm, "What happened to the buggy?"

Rachel took over from the Bishop, while he explained to the stranger exactly what had happened, and suggested that they come to recover the buggy in the morning once the rain has passed.

"Betty, you will have to get on the horse with Amity, Rachel you will walk with Uri and I," the Bishop instructed and then the stranger named Uri, helped Amity, and then Betty on to the horse.

Together they slowly made their way back to society, the first stop was Amity's house, where the Bishop helped to get her inside, and seen to, then it was Rachel's turn and finally Uri, Bishop Gunther and Betty made their way to the Bishop's house.

~*~

After Rachel had changed into her night dress and towel dried her wet hair, she deposited herself in front of the fire place. The night had turned out a complete disaster. She was sure it was punishment for their bad behaviour. Lusting like that over fictitious men and so on. She wrapped her quilt around her shoulders and reached for her bible. She knew better than to let her judgement be influenced by anyone. Despite the guilt, she somehow found her mind drifting to the stranger who came to their aid. She still couldn't see his face clearly, but she was sure he was handsome, and strong.

She shook her head to chase away the thoughts and closed her eyes, and said a silent prayer of repentance. She was never going to look at those magazines again.

Chapter 2

The sun broke through the parted curtains in Rachel's room and she pinched her eyes shut. The night before had taken its toll on her, and resulted in her oversleeping when there was still so much to do. She was yet to feed the geese and get ready to go to the local market to deliver the eggs she had collected the day before, but she simply had no will power.

"Rachel!" Her step-mother called from the kitchen, "Come have your breakfast!"

Rachel covered her eyes with her forearm and sighed. She just needed a few more minutes of sleep, but she knew where her priorities lay. She willed herself out of bed and rushed around the room to get ready for the day. By the time she got to the kitchen her mother had already cleaned the dishes, and Rachel's breakfast was waiting.

"The Bishop and his friend were here earlier," Elsa commented in passing, "Looks like you girls had a rough night."

"Yeah, we got caught in the storm," she mumbled.

So the stranger is one of the Bishop's friends, which means he was old, she thought to herself.

"Apparently Amity had twisted her ankle quite badly, but she will be fine in a few days."

"I figured. She stepped in a hole when she tried to get out of the buggy, we couldn't see much."

Elsa came to sit at the table with her, "You girls need to be more careful, things could have been a lot worse."

Sometimes Rachel couldn't help but wonder what Elsa's agenda really was. At times she treated her like a stranger, barely paying attention to her, and other times she came across all motherly. And all this time Rachel had no choice but to keep her own emotions all bottled up.

"We will," Rachel said and stood up to wash her plate, "I'm taking the eggs to the market, is there anything you need me to do?"

"Oh not to worry about the eggs, I've already sold delivered them this morning."

Rachel felt as if she could crush the plate in her hands. Those eggs were her eggs, her income. She was saving money for herself, and now Elsa had taken the little bit she could earn for herself.

"Thank you," she said tight lipped without turning around.

"I hope you don't mind, your father does need some money to buy that new gas stove so, I figured every penny would help."

"Of course," Rachel turned around this time, with a fake smile plastered on her face, "I'll just get more eggs to get money for my new dress."

"Why on earth would you need a new dress?" Elsa said with mock surprise, "Don't you have enough as it is?"

Rachel was slowly starting to lose her temper, but she fought hard to remain calm, "I only have three dresses, and I need one for church, the others are all worn and faded."

Elsa laughed, "It's not like you'll be catching anyone's eye, and you're past the point of marriage. You're already considered a spinster."

"I'm only twenty-two, the same age my mother married," Rachel protested.

"And see how that turned out."

Elsa had barely said the words when her sons, Caleb and Alfred came into the kitchen, and Rachel had to hide her anger. She simply scooped up her empty egg baskets and stormed out of the house. How that woman dared say such heartless things and get away with it, was beyond her she thought as she marched determinedly in no particular direction. But as the anger subsided, it was replaced by doubt. Maybe it was too late for her to marry, but then the same applied to Betty and Amity, they were both the same age. Obviously living in Derby Creek wasn't much help either, there were far more women than men here, and unless they had gatherings from nearby towns, chances of finding a suitor was slim.

First of all there was Betty, who insisted that she was waiting for Mr Right, she refused to settle for less, then there's Amity who also had her own ideas of a suitor, and the few men that did ask for her hand in the past, were coldly turned down because she was just not interested. Rachel always thought that Amity was the kind who would go on a Rumspringa if her father allowed her, out of the three friends, she was the adventurous one.

Rachel grunted a loud oomph as she collided with someone sending her baskets flying. Thankfully they were empty; otherwise they would both have been covered in egg yolk. She stumbled back and started to apologize profusely when she swallowed her words, and a pair of very strong hands cupped her shoulders.

"Are you alight?" the young man asked, and offered her a lopsided smile.

"Jah, I am fine, I-I wasn't paying attention, I'm sorry," she said struggling to breathe.

"It's quite alright, you were miles away there for a second, I'm Uri, Rachel right?" he said and released her as he tucked his thumbs into his suspenders.

Uri, the name immediately rang a bell. He was Bishop Gunther's friend, but how? He was so young, she wondered.

"How do you know my name?" she asked foolishly.

"I came to your rescue last night in the storm, but I suppose you won't recognise me, it was rather dark."

"Oh! Oh right, yes. Well... um, I'll be going now. Thank you, I mean sorry, I... I have to go."

Rachel just about ran away from him, she had acted like a complete and utter fool, stuttering over her words like a second grader having to do an oral assignment. No wonder she was single. She couldn't sit in the company of a man without feeling awkward. As she hurried away she could feel his eyes burn into the back of her, but she refused to glance back. The farther she got away the quicker her out of control heart and raging butterflies would quieten down.

"Rachel!" It was Betty who waved her down, "Where are you heading?"

"Eggs!"

"You're going to Eggs?" Betty giggled.

"No, ugh, I'm going to collect eggs silly," she corrected herself as Betty fell into step next to her, "How is Amity doing?"

"She's fine, but you look like you've seen a ghost, why are you in such a hurry," Betty said as she tried to keep up to Rachel's pace.

"I need to sell enough eggs to buy a new dress. The cow sold all the eggs I collected yesterday."

"What a cow, did she not even ask you?"

"Does she ever?"

The rest of the way, the two friends walked in silence, Betty on her own planet, and Rachel trying to get Uri out of her mind. She hadn't expected him to be so young, nor did she expect him to know her name. The night before was a bit of a blur with everything going on, and she mostly remembered walking beside Bishop Gunther while Uri guided the horse by its reins with Amity and Betty on horseback.

"Is Uri your..."

"Don't you think Uri is..."

They both said at the same time and then burst out laughing.

"Uri is so handsome," Betty continued, "The last time I saw him was when we were kids. His family has been in Germany for the past few years."

"I didn't expect him to be so young," Rachel said, "Are they staying here?"

"Only Uri, he's staying at our house and is helping papa with a few things."

Rachel could hear by Betty's tone that she was keen on Uri, and she knew by the seam of her dress, that Amity will be just as taken by him.

One of them will most certainly catch his eyes, she thought and smiled softly. Her friends or at least one of them deserved a good strong man to care for them.

She dismissed the notion of Uri straight away, knowing that she would never stand a chance. She could hardly string together a proper sentence when she bumped into him earlier.

Chapter 3

Amity humped along with a crutch in one hand, while Betty excitedly skipped besides them. For the first time in who knows how long, Betty and Amity had made some effort to look presentable, both of them had brand new dresses. It was the Friday night frolic, where most boys got to voice their intentions.

Betty was nervous; as usual she was shy and nervous. She never liked these events much, she did not trust the thing called love, her father loved once, he had promised his her mother that he would make sure she was taken care of, but now years later, all she had to remember her mother by was a single letter, and a lifetime of regret. Elsa was kind in some ways, but she was jealous of Betty, and Betty never did much right in her eyes.

The people from the surrounding farms started to arrive, old and young, in the middle of the big barn the table was set as always. Food in excess was spread across the table, along with lanterns casting a dim glow over everything.

"Have you seen how handsome Uri is?" Betty whispered under her breath.

Amity giggled and shifted in her chair, "I know right? I can still feel his hands on my hips as he helped me on to the horse."

"Oh and weren't they the biggest stronger hands ever?" Betty swooned.

"I'm going to make a play for him you know?" Amity murmured under her breath.

"No you're not, I am, and I've already spent some quality time with him."

Betty wagged her brows and reached for bunch of grapes.

"You can't eat now, we have to say thanks first," Amity said slapping Betty's hand.

"Oh please, no one is even looking."

Betty listened to her friends as they cooed over the newcomer and she opted not to show any interest. They had reason to try and win his affection, she had none. She will see this night through and make the best of a bad situation. Besides, she had a lot more on her mind. Maybe it was time she accepted the fact that she was a spinster, and she figured it was time she spoke to the Bishop and go his take on her moving out of her paternal home into her own. She could always offer her help as a teacher. She knew how to read, in fact she loved reading. She could go spend time at the local school and read to the youngsters, even help the school teachers to give extra lessons in literacy.

"Rachel!" Amity's voice broke into her thoughts.

"Oh... sorry I wasn't listening," she apologised.

"I was saying, maybe all three of us should play for Uri, we can see which one he picks."

Rachel raised her brows, "He's not up for auction, it's a silly game you're wanting to play."

"Stop being such a drab! It will be fun."

No it won't, she thought. The first thing that is bound to happen is that Uri will pick either Betty or Amity, then that will leave one or the other angry and disappointed, ruining a friendship of many years.

"I'm not a drab, I'm just saying. What if he picks Betty, then you'll be angry, not?"

Amity rolled her eyes, "You take things way to seriously, if he picks Betty, then so be it, I'm hardly desperate to marry."

"Come on Rachel, it will be fun; besides, maybe he shows no interest in any of us, then at least we know we all tried."

Betty worried her lip and looked down at her hands, "I don't know, I suppose no harm can come of it." She for one knew that she won't be the least bit phased if he picked Amity or Betty, because she knew she stood no chance.

Amity shoved her elbow into Rachel's ribs and gestured with her head towards the door. Talk of the devil, Uri was heading straight down the path on the opposite side of the table with his eyes fixed on them. And once again the sight of him made her heart race and as she watched him approach it was as if all else around her faded. She had tunnel vision and it was only him looking straight at her. When he finally stopped and took a seat directly opposite her she averted her eyes immediately. Of course, Amity kicked her under the table and Rachel cleared her throat uncomfortably.

"*Hallo* Uri," she said.

"*Hoe gaan het*, Rachel?" he smiled.

She only nodded, her tongue felt like led in her mouth, and her palms were sweaty.

Betty and Amity both fell right into conversation, putting their best foot forward while Rachel wanted nothing but to flee. Soon enough the evening got on the way, with youngsters all frolicking and enjoying the event. Uri made sure he mingled with everyone and never let on that he was interested in any of them in particular, which was funny, since Betty put her best foot forward and out rightly told him he had beautiful eyes.

As the evening drew to a close and most of the people had left, the last remaining few spent the rest of the time talking about the up and coming barn raising event. Uri was still seated across from Rachel, and Betty and Amity had moved closer to where Bishop Gunther was. He was playing the harmonica, which was probably the only instrument allowed in the community, but still sounded like heaven.

"So Rachel, have you always lived here?" Uri asked curiously as he picked on some of the bread sticks on his plate.

"*Jah*, I was born here," she said and offered him a shy smile.

"I'm surprised I don't remember you?"

"I'm not exactly the most memorable of all," she laughed.

"Oh but you are, you are a very beautiful woman."

Rachel blushed profusely and covered the side of her face with her hand, "Thank you," she mumbled.

"Can I pick you up for church on Sunday?"

Shocked at his request, Rachel shifted uncomfortably in her seat and worried her lip, as tempting as it was, she wasn't so sure if it was a good idea. But then again, Betty and Amity did say that they should all try and win his affection. She looked down at her empty plate and smiled. Perhaps it was time she stepped out of her comfort zone and tried dating at least, after all, he was simply going to take her to church, and it wasn't like he was proposing to her at all.

"Sure," she said and then got up, "I have to go now. I will see you around."

She saw his mouth open and close, but she rushed away regardless. She said her goodbyes to her friends and the rest of the community who were all still in the barn and headed home. Her mind was racing and her heart even more. For the life of her she couldn't understand what Uri saw in her. *You're a beautiful woman* – he had said, and it made her feel as if she was about to fly into the night sky on wings of angels. No boy, or man for that matter, had ever paid her such a compliment, and coming from someone as handsome and Uri, made her tummy do strange things.

Chapter 4

Uri was up and ready long before dawn on Sunday, making sure his buggy was clean and that he too was dressed in his best church clothes. He couldn't deny the fact that he felt bad for Betty, she had shown her affection so openly, but there was just no chemistry between them. Unlike Rachel, Betty was just too flamboyant to his liking. She was a pretty woman, but not even nearly as pretty as Rachel. Rachel was unusually pretty, with red hair that always seemed so perfectly plated and rolled up under her prayer cap, with loose strands that tickled her cheeks. The slight dusting of freckles across her nose, that spread to her cheeks made her even prettier, almost innocent not to mention the way she blushed every time he spoke to her.

He was quite surprised when she accepted his request to start off with, but pleased nonetheless.

The first night he saw the shy girl, with her baskets filled with eggs, he was intrigued. She was in control despite the stormy weather and their predicament, and even when he lifted the other two on to the horse, she never uttered as single complaint. She walked quietly next to them as if she was taking a stroll. Not even the rain slanting heavily against them broke through her composure. Maybe it was the way she kept to herself, or the way her eyes lit up the next day when he bumped into her, he wasn't quite sure himself, but if he had to pin it to one thing, it was God's will. It was God's will that he returned to Derby Creek after all these years and God had sent the storm so that he could meet his future wife.

"Uri, you're up early," Betty said as she entered the kitchen where he was having his morning tea.

"Jah, up and ready for church," he said and grinned excitedly.

She came to sit next to him and perched her chin on her hand, looking at him all dreamy eyed. Shifting slightly to get some distance, he smiled and shoved the plate of rusks closer to her.

"I'm on my way to collect Rachel for church," he announced, not sure how Betty would react.

From day one, she had made it no secret that she fancied him; neither did Amity, so it was better if he got it out in the open before either of them got their hopes up.

"Rachel?" Betty said scrunching up her face, "Have you asked her then?"

He nodded and took the last sip of his tea, "Jah, she's a shy one, but she accepted my offer."

Betty scratched her head and slumped back in her chair, and Uri could just imagine what thoughts were flitting through her mind, hoping that this would not ruin their friendship. But when Betty stood up and held her hand up for a high-five, he grinned.

"She's a dear friend, but a nervous wreck, you best make sure you treat her right," Betty grinned, "She's had a lot of hardship with that stepmother of hers."

Uri frowned, tempted to ask about this stepmother, but held back. If anyone was going to tell him about Rachel, it was Rachel herself. He would want for no secrets or tall tales to come from anyone other than her.

He looked at the clock against the wall in the kitchen and took his hat, nodded at Betty and headed out. For a man nearing his thirties, he felt like teenager himself.

~*~

Rachel waited outside for Uri's arrival and her stomach was doing wild flips, while her heart was missing beats every so often trying to keep up the pace. She had never entertained the advances of a man, and had no idea how to behave in the presence of one who had made his intensions clear. A boy simply did not offer a girl a ride in his buggy unless he was interested in her as more than a friend. This was serious business. She also omitted to let her father know, because she knew that Elsa would have a hundred and one things to say about it. She shifted on the swing chair changing her position, trying to find the one that made her feel most at ease, but her body felt awkward. Her arms felt as if they were too long, her legs felt numb and overall her body and mind appeared to be disconnected. Tired of trying to figure out the best seating position she stood up and paced up and down the porch, and then finally she opted for leaning against the pillar. Just in time too, as she heard the nearing rumble of a buggy, which could only have been Uri.

When he came to a stop in front of her gate, she quickly rushed down the stairs.

"Morning Rachel, you look lovely today," Uri said as he climbed out and came around to help her in.

"Good morning," she said softly.

"Did you sleep well?"

"Jah, I did, thank you."

It took her some time to loosen up and say more than four words at a time, but Uri had this amazing ability to make her feel free. With him she didn't have to count every word, or watch her tongue. She could just say what she wanted. On their way to church, he asked her about the things she likes most. The talked about her life, and her family, she didn't feel like she needed to hide anything from him at all. She even admitted how she felt about Elsa, which made her feel less restricted. At church, they didn't sit next to each other, but Betty and Amity were curious as ever.

"So he picked you did he?" Amity whispered under her breath.

"I don't know, maybe," Rachel murmured.

"You're blind as a bat; everyone can see he likes you."

Rachel blushed and kept her head down, her friends were impossible and as much as she tried to pay attention to the service she couldn't. If it wasn't for Betty or Amity, whispering to her under their breaths, it was the sure awareness of Uri watching her. And that did not go unnoticed by her friends either.

By the time the service had come to an end, Rachel couldn't wait to get outside to catch a breath of fresh air, and steal a moment for herself, but it was short lived.

"You never told us you're meeting a boy?" Elsa said as she came to stand next to Rachel.

"I didn't know I needed your permission," Rachel said blankly.

"Well I suppose you are old enough to make your own, but you know, Albert will be very disappointed that you never told him."

Rachel knew exactly what Elsa was playing at, and this time she was not going to let the woman who pretends to care throw any hurdles in her way.

"I think he'll live, and you should be too pleased that I won't be a bother to you for much longer."

Talk about rushing into things, Rachel thought as she hurried away from Elsa, it wasn't as if Uri was going to ask for her hand in marriage, they hardly knew each other. But even if that wasn't the case, whatever happened, come the beginning of winter, she would move out anyway and start her own life, with or without a husband.

Chapter 5

Uri had spent most of the time getting to know Rachel, and the more he got to know her, the more he was convinced that she was the perfect wife for him. He had spent almost every evening visiting with Rachel and in the past few months since they started their courtship he got to know a woman, who despite her adversities in life, rose above it all. Her stepmother no longer tried to boss her around, and her father was too pleased that his only daughter is finally blooming.

It was a perfect autumn day; the ground was covered in a carpet of reds and golds that reminded him of Rachel. He had already asked her father for her hand in marriage, and although it didn't quite follow the custom of dating for an extended period, he saw no reason to wait. They were both adults who were in love and certain of one thing, their own happiness.

As usual he waited patiently for Rachel to exit the house, and like two curious toddlers Amity and Betty was not far away either. They had both come to terms with the fact that he had made his choice, and they were extra supportive of Rachel too. As he whispered a silent prayer for guidance, Rachel made her appearance as if the Lord had answered his prayer. Today was the day he was going to ask her for her hand in person.

"Good morning Uri," she said and her smile lit up his world.

"Morning to you Rachel, you look absolutely radiant today," he complemented her and it earned him an even wider smile.

"I made myself a new dress, do you like it?"

"It's beautiful," he said and held out his hand.

He could already imagine the gasps and giggles coming from the two friends as he struggled to find the right words. He had rehearsed it so well, but now here in the moment, he was at a loss for words.

"Are you alright?" she asked and placed the back of her hand against his cheek, "You look flustered."

Uri cleared his throat and caught her hand, keeping it against his cheek, "I'm fine, but there is something I would like to ask you."

Rachel tilted her head and her hazel eyes sparkled with curiosity as she waited for him to speak.

"Go on!" Betty shouted from across the road!

Uri closed his eyes and smiled, they weren't helping him at all.

"Uri?" Rachel said softly, "What is it?"

He took a deep breath, and then took both her hands in his, "Rachel, I have spoken to your father, and I would be honoured if you would agree to become my wife."

The way Rachel's expression changed from being concerned to completely surprise was priceless. She didn't have to answer him at all, because the way her lips tugged into a wide smile and her eyes filled with tears, he knew she wouldn't turn him down.

Rachel flung her arms around his neck and buried her face in the crook of his neck and whispered, "I thought you'd never ask."

Uri chuckled, "I was hoping you would accept."

"Why would I not?" she said and smiled lovingly up at him.

RUMSPRINGA ROMANCE

DEIDRA SCOTT

BOOK ONE

Chapter One

Leah Eicher opened one eye and peered around her bedroom. The new morning sun was softly streaming in through the window, lighting up the small room. Leah's younger sister, Amanda, was still soundly sleeping in the other twin bed. In some ways, Leah was happy to have a few minutes to herself, but she also battled an intense urge to wake her sister so that she could share her excitement with someone else.

Today was Leah's birthday.

Sixteen-years-old.

This was the day that Leah had waited for since she was a little girl. In her Kentucky Amish community, sixteen was a turning point in a girl's life. While Leah wouldn't be getting a driver's license like the *Englisher* girls her age, she would now be able to start attending the young peoples' gatherings. These gatherings were where the Amish teenagers and young adults spent time together and paired off with dates who would eventually become their husbands and wives.

"Ugh..." Leah heard Amanda let out a groan and turned to watch her sister stretch her arms over her head, "Is it morning already?"

"Amanda," Lead scurried out of her bed and practically jumped to her sister's side, "Do you know what today is?"

Amanda closed her eyes and let out a yawn, "Sunday, I think."

"Do you know what that means?"

Suddenly Amanda's eyes shot open and her face broke out in a gigantic smile, "Oh, Leah, is this really the day?! Happy birthday sister!"

Sitting up in bed, Amanda reach out to grab her older sister in a hug.

"Today truly is my sixteenth birthday!" Leah announced with a grin as she tucked a strand of long black hair behind her ear, "I can't believe it's really here!"

"I can't either!" Amanda let out a moan, "Oh, I am so jealous of you, Leah! I can hardly wait until I can go to the young peoples' gatherings!"

Leah jumped to her feet and started to unbutton her nightgown so she could get dressed for church, "But you have to wait two more years."

Amanda tossed a pillow at her sister with a laugh, "Don't rub it in! It feels like sixteen can't get here soon enough. Oh, Leah, you've got to promise not to stay out too late....or else I may fall asleep before I get to hear every detail about what happens! Oh, what do you think will happen? Do you think you might possibly meet a beau this soon?"

Leah grinned, "I can't wish for a serious boyfriend this fast, but I certainly hope I get a nice looking ride home from the gathering."

"What about Enos Troyer?" Amanda asked with a giggle.

Just the name of the handsome boy made Leah start to blush. Enos was three years older than Leah, but she had been madly in love with him for years. The Troyer family had moved into the community four years earlier and, even in all that time, Leah and Enos had never had a chance to get to know each other. How Leah hoped that might change now that she was old enough to be included in the young peoples' events!

"*Ach*, Amanda," she scolded her sister as she sat back down on the side of her bed, well aware that her face was red with embarrassment, "Don't you dare tell a soul, but I certainly hope so! I can't think of anyone I'd rather spend time with than Enos."

"Enos and Leah Troyer," Amanda drew out the name with a naughty smirk, her dark eyes gleaming with mischief.

"Hush now!" Leah exclaimed, throwing a pillow back at her, "I don't want *Mamm* and *Daed* to hear that one!" Leah couldn't decide if she was more embarrassed or excited as she whispered back, "But it does sound good, doesn't it?"

Both girls burst into laughter, giggling until they heard their father's loud voice, calling them to start getting ready for church.

Leah could hardly concentrate during the sermon. Although she wanted to pay attention, she was too giddy and her mind continued to wander to the day ahead of her. Once the service was finished, the entire community would gather to eat a delicious meal out in the yard. Once the dishes were cleared and everything tidied up, families would start to leave, giving the young people a chance to spend time alone together.

Sometimes the young peoples' gatherings included board games, singing old German songs as a group, and enjoying a good meal.

Leah glanced across the room, trying to seek out Enos Troyer. There he sat next to his *daed*. He was staring at the preacher intently, giving Leah a chance to watch him.

My, what a good looking young man! He was tall and thin yet muscular. His jaw was solid and rugged, his hair the color of the silk Leah was used to shucking off the corn, and his eyes a penetrating blue.

Leah shook her head slowly, trying to rid her thoughts of Enos. She would have a chance to spend time with him tonight, but waiting seemed to be taking an eternity.

After the service was finished, the Amish slowly began to file out of the house so that they could prepare for the large community picnic.

Leah and her family were starting out the front door when they encountered Leah's grandfather.

"Hey *Daed*," Leah's father greeted his own dad with a pat on the shoulder, "I didn't see ya during the service. You must have slipped in."

Despite the fact that Grandpa Matthew was only in his early sixties, time was taking a toll on his appearance. Rather than standing tall, he was now stooped over and he seemed to be losing weight. Leah studied his face and realized that Grandpa Matthew's eyes were red and there were tear marks down his cheeks.

"*Ach*, Joe," Grandpa Matthew spoke to Leah's father, "You know I can't leave your *mamm* home alone for long. I had one of the nurses come to watch her so I could come to church, but she got there late. I had to slip in the back once the service had already started."

"How is Mom today?" Leah could hear the concern in her dad's voice.

Grandpa Matthew shrugged his shoulders and clutched tighter against the black felt hat he held in his hands, "About the same, I suppose."

For the past year, Grandma Bessie had been fighting a nasty battle with cancer. Despite treatment, it seemed that she was only going to get worse. Leah had heard her parents talking together, speculating that she wouldn't make it to winter.

"Would you like to sit with us today, Dad?" Leah's father asked, pointing out toward one of the picnic tables where some of the Amish women were starting to put out plates of freshly baked bread, potato salad, noodles, and baked chicken.

Grandpa Matthew slowly shook his head, "Not today. I need to get back home."

"A break might do you good!" Leah's mother suggested, "Give yourself a chance to relax, to get away from your troubles."

"Bessie might need me." With that, Grandpa Matthew put his hat on his head and went out the door toward his buggy.

Leah looked up at her father's sad face. She knew it hurt him to see his dad suffer so.

"Leah," he took a deep breath, "Tomorrow I want you to take some food out to your grandpa and see if you can help him for a bit. He's working far too hard."

Leah nodded her head obediently. A quiet man, she had never known much about her grandfather; however, as long as the visit could be short, she wouldn't mind checking on him occasionally.

Matthew Eicher finished unhitching his buggy and started toward his house. He had built the large white farm-house forty-four years ago right after he and Bessie were married. Together they had weathered many storms in that house, including the death of two babies and the raising of ten other children who were now adults with families of their own.

When Matthew stepped in the back door, he could hear the nurse he had hired punching away at buttons on her phone.

"Oh, hey, Mr. Eicher!" She exclaimed as she hurried to turn off the game she had been playing and stuffed the device down in her purse, "That was really quick!"

"How's she doing?"

The nurse smiled sweetly as she smacked away at a piece of chewing gum, "She slept the whole time you were gone."

Matthew took a deep breath as he reached in his pocket and pulled out the right change to pay the nurse for her time.

"Thanks Mr. Eicher. See you sometime soon!" She flashed Matthew a big smile and hurried out the door to her fancy red car.

As soon as she was gone, Matthew made his way into the bedroom where Bessie was soundly sleeping in the hospital bed he had recently purchased. On a nearby nightstand were endless bottles of pills along with doctor notes and appointment reminder cards.

For many years, that room had been a place of sanctuary. When Matthew had come home from a hard day's work, he had looked forward to relaxing in his bedroom, listening to the crickets through the open window, and releasing all of his frustrations as he poured his heart out to his wife.

But somewhere along the way, everything had changed. The room was no longer a place of refuge; instead, it was a painful reminder of a marriage that had disintegrated before his very eyes.

Looking at his wife's gaunt form lying under a thin white sheet, Matthew had to wipe another tear from his eye.

Bessie had deserved so much better. She deserved a husband who had loved her, who would share everything with her, a husband who would be her teammate. What had she gotten? A husband who only focused on his own pleasure, a man who ultimately let his work become the center of his life and left his wife alone.

Now, Matthew discovered that he was an old man, torn apart by bitterness, regrets, and guilt. He wanted so badly to ask his wife for forgiveness but, now that so much time had passed, it was hard to tell her anything at all.

Ach, Matthew, he whispered to himself, *best to just leave it be.*

No matter how much he wanted things to be different, they weren't and they never could be. He had cheated Bessie out of a happy life and now there was no way to turn back the hands of time and right his wrongs.

Leah settled down for the Sunday meal with her family. Although she had loaded her plate full of the yummy-good food, she was so nervous and anxious that she could hardly swallow.

It seemed that overnight her entire life had changed. Suddenly, she had become a young woman and anything was possible. All the romance books she had loved to read throughout the years could now become her reality.

"Hey Leah!"

She practically jumped when she heard someone's voice speak up behind her.

Turning, she saw Luke Schmidt awkwardly standing near their table, a plate of food held in one hand.

"Oh, hello, Luke," Leah said with a smile. Although Luke was several years old than her, Leah had spent a lot of time at his house last summer, helping him *mamm* out after his twin brothers were born.

Although he was usually quiet and kept to himself, Luke seemed to have developed some what of a friendship with Leah during that time. Each morning he would pick her up at her house and each afternoon he would give her a ride home on his parents' buggy.

"Happy birthday, Leah," Luke spoke softly with a smile playing on the corner of his lips.

"Oh, *dank*i!" Leah exclaimed, surprised that he had even thought of it, "I didn't think anyone realized it was my birthday."

"Are you going to the young peoples' gathering tonight?"

Leah nodded her head, "Oh yes! Are you?"

Luke shrugged slowly, "I don't go a lot, but I think I will tonight." He opened his mouth as if he wanted to say something else but then gave a smile, "See ya later, Leah."

As soon as Luke was out of earshot, Leah noticed Amanda smirking and holding back a laugh.

"What's wrong with you?" Leah asked, almost afraid to know the answer.

Amanda shook her head and muttered, "That man is all mush for you, Leah."

"*Ach*," Leah snorted and took a deep breath, "He better not be!"

Although Luke was a nice enough boy, he certainly was not the one who would fulfill Leah's dreams of a fairytale romance. Shorter than the rest of the young men, Luke was also a good deal heavier. His face was pudgy and round, more like a teddy bear than a dashing suitor.

"I don't think he's quite Prince Charming, do you?" Leah whispered back.

Amanda almost choked on her bite of chicken as she replied, "Luke and Leah Schmidt. Judging by his size, you'd better be a good cook if you want to keep him happy!"

Leah raised an eyebrow but chose to avoid making a scene that her father might overhear. Her dad wasn't one to ignore what he considered foolishness among his children.

Glancing through the crowds of Amish, she searched for Enos.

Luke had better not have any ideas about her because, as far as Leah was concerned, she was already taken by Enos Troyer.

Chapter Two

The warm early June afternoon quickly turned to the chilly side once the sun started to go down over the hills. Leah's family had gone back home right after the meal, leaving her to find her own way back to their house after the gathering was over.

While waiting for the evening's events to start, Leah had spent time visiting with Suzie Scholfus. Suzie's parents were hosting the gathering out in their barn.

Since Suzie was only fifteen, she would have to stay inside and wait her turn just like everyone else.

As soon as evening started to close in, buggies began pulling into the Scholfus lane. As Leah watched out Suzie's bedroom window, she felt a thrill of excitement run down her spine.

"Oh, Leah, aren't you scared?" Suzie asked as she put aside a book that they had been reading together.

Leah couldn't help but nod her head, "*Ach,* I wish not, but I certainly am!"

Suzie hurried to Leah's side and grabbed one of her hands in her own, "Can't you imagine that it will be just like the book that we've been reading? You'll be in that crowd of young people and, suddenly, you will notice a man who will one day become your husband!"

They both let out a squeal of excitement at the idea.

Being sixteen was even better than Leah had imagined!

When Leah finally gathered the courage to make her way out to the barn, a crowd of Amish boys and girls had already congregated inside. The bright lanterns made the barn light even in the darkness of the evening. Several couples had already paired off to talk, while another group of girls spent their time chatting together and the boys were playing a game of darts against the barn wall.

The other girls were so excited to finally have Leah among their number. They were anxious to group around her, chattering on about books that they had been reading, dresses they had been sewing, and the antics of their playful brothers and sisters.

Although Leah had fun among her friends, she was almost disappointed to realize that the young peoples' gathering wasn't going to provide an instant romantic fairytale. She spent most of her time looking through the crowd, trying to keep an eye out for Enos.

"Hello again, Leah!" She hadn't even realized that the other girls had moved on to play a board game when she heard a familiar voice by her side. It was no surprise when she looked to see Luke standing to her right, one of Mrs. Scholfus' cookies in his hand.

"Oh, hello, Luke. I see you made it."

Luke nodded his head and smiled, "Of course I did. I'm nineteen but I've only come to a handful of these things before. I'm afraid I'm not much of one for socializing." After an moment of silence, he went on to say, "I saw your grandpa in church today. How's your granny doing?"

"Oh," Leah gave a shrug, "She's doing about the same, I guess. Grandpa Matthew seems to be having a rough time of it, though. He has so much work trying to keep up with the farm and now with Granny Bessie sick he not only has additional work but a lot of extra bills. The community is helping with the hospital costs, but he still has to pay for a nurse to help him sometimes and also for someone to drive them to their appointments."

Luke sighed and shook his head, "I hate to hear that. Your Grandpa Matthew has always been a good man."

Leah didn't like thinking about her grandparents, so she changed the subject, "How are the twins doing?"

"Ah, they're wild now that they can walk! My *mamm* says that they're the worst she's had yet. Yesterday I was pulling them around in the little red wagon after work..."

Although Luke kept talking about the wild antics of his mischievous brothers, it was hard for Leah to listen. She was much too busy looking for Enos to want to hear boring tales about little children.

Suddenly, she spotted him walking into the barn. Several of the boys were bringing in additional benches, each holding onto an end and working together; however, Enos was carrying one of the heavy wooden benches entirely by himself. My, was he ever strong!

"It was nice to see you, Luke," Leah spoke up, suddenly cutting him short in his story. With that, she carefully made her way across the barn, trying to get closer to Enos.

Each minute that passed was another she should be spending trying to get to know this handsome young man.

Leah spent the entire night trying to stay close to Enos Troyer, but it seemed that, every chance that she had to even stand by his side, he was off with someone else. Enos was the life of the party and all the young people were anxious to spend time with him. Leah was beginning to realize that, most likely, catching Enos wasn't going to be as easy as she had initially hoped! Her plans of an instant romance were seeming more far-out as she watched him flirt with all the other girls, but not give so much as a glance in her direction.

As the hours passed, the young folks started to pair off to travel back home. Several of her friends found Leah and offered her a ride home with them, but she turned them all down. Until all hope was gone, she would wait on any chance to speak to Enos. There was still a tiny sliver of possibility that he would notice her and offer to give her a ride home, and she would not give up before that last chance was gone.

The Scholfus family had put out a wide variety of delicious snacks on a table in the middle of the barn. As Leah went over to pick up a cookie, she found herself face-to-face with none other than Enos Troyer.

"Oh, hello," she gasped, trying to gain her composure as a flock of butterflies took flight in her stomach, "I didn't see you there. How are you, Enos?"

Enos looked at her in surprise, "You're Joe Eicher's daughter, right?"

Something about the question was almost insulting. Although Enos' family was fairly new to the community, he should certainly know her by now.

Leah tried to smile, "Yes, it's Leah."

There was silence for a moment and Leah found herself looking down at the snacks that were still left on the table.

"You look rather lonely tonight!" Enos suddenly announced, "Would you like a ride home?"

Leah's heart skipped a beat as she looked up in surprise. Would she ever?! She wanted to say yes, but her mouth wouldn't work right.

"Of course, Enos!" Another voice spoke up and Leah realized that Katie Hershbarger had also joined them at the snack table.

With that, Enos led Katie out to his buggy.

Watching them walk away, Leah felt her heart sink. The disappointment of it all mingled with the excitement of the day was almost too much for her to handle. She reached up and gently wiped a tear away from her cheek.

Looking around, she realized that almost everyone had left and she would have no way to get home. She dreaded the idea of trudging across the road to the phone shanty so that she could call a driver to take her back to her parents' house.

"I'm about to leave, would ya like to come with me?"

Leah recognized the voice immediately. Luke Schmidt. She didn't know if she should cry more or just be thankful for any ride at all.

"That would be so nice," she heard herself muttering, "I'm afraid this has been a little bit too much for me. I'm awful tired."

Matthew Eicher awoke with a jump. He had fallen asleep fully clothed and sitting in a chair beside his bed.

Standing up, he went to Bessie's side. Somehow, he simply felt as if something was wrong.

In the darkness, he tried to watch for the rise and fall of her chest, but saw nothing.

"Bessie," he whispered, dreading the worst, "Bessie!"

Suddenly, he saw his wife move her arm and let out a little moan.

Matthew stepped back and put his hand against his forehead. He was breathing so hard, he felt like his heart was pounding in his chest like an Indian drum.

He thought he had lost her.

He couldn't lose her. Not now. Not the way that things were.

Bessie couldn't go without knowing the truth.

But one day he would lose her and, if he didn't find his courage soon, he knew that he'd never be able to do it.

Matthew sat down hard on the bed and covered his face with his hands.

He had to apologize, but doing so might kill him right along with his wife.

The drive home from the young peoples' gathering was silent for the most part. Luke tried to make some small talk, but Leah didn't feel like chiming in. She had never known rejection before, and experiencing it hurt so much more than she had ever imagined.

"I'm sorry," she finally muttered as Luke pulled his horse up in front of her family's two-story house, "I haven't been very good company tonight. I'm afraid that this night wore me out more than I expect."

Luke cocked his head and looked at her, studying her with his blue eyes.

"You know," Luke finally announced, "The get-togethers aren't for everybody. There's no shame in just not liking them."

Something about his words hit Leah the wrong way. It annoyed her to think that Luke would try to understand her or simply take her as anti-social.

Leah nodded soberly, "I suppose I'm just not used to them."

"It will be more fun next time," Luke suggested, obviously searching for anything to make her feel better, "You've got two whole weeks to wait, though!"

Leah tried to smile, "*Danke* for the ride, Luke. I appreciate it a lot."

"See ya, Leah."

Leah hurried into the house, quietly opening the door and tiptoeing to her bedroom. She could only hope that everyone was asleep and would stay that way.

Closing her bedroom door softly, Leah reached for her nightgown and started to get ready for bed.

"Who brought you home?"

Leah felt her heart fall when she heard the sound of her sister's voice speak out in the darkness. She had at least hoped for one night to cry in peace before she had to speak her troubles out-loud.

"Was it Enos?"

Leah shook her head and took a deep breath, "Oh, Amanda, the night was a disaster! I hardly got to speak to Enos at all! I thought that he was asking to give me a ride, but then it turned out he was talking to someone else...and I ended up riding home with Luke Schmidt."

Amanda couldn't hold back her laugh, even though she took a pillow and held it against her face.

"*Ach*, Leah," she finally managed to say once she got done laughing, "I'm not quite so jealous now. Did you give him a goodnight kiss?"

Leah scooted into bed and pulled the covers tight under her chin.

"Amanda," she hissed bitterly, "I am certainly not in the mood!"

Her sixteenth birthday had been a disaster and, try as she might, Leah couldn't keep the tears from pouring down her cheeks. If this was the way that the young peoples' gatherings were going to be, Leah wasn't sure she ever wanted to go back!

Chapter Three

The next morning, Leah's father insisted that she make good on her promise to go see her grandparents. Leah and her mother baked a delicious meal of potato soup, fresh bread, and apple pie to take along.

"Now," Leah's mother advised as she put the food together in a basket, "I don't want you to just drop the food and run. You stay there and visit with your Grandpa Matthew for a while. I know you don't like him much..."

"I like Grandma Bessie better," Leah interrupted, "But seeing her sick makes me so sad! I've never enjoyed Grandpa. He's also so dreary, and now he's worse than ever! Being there simply makes me depressed."

Leah's mom raised an eyebrow, "That's not love, Leah, that's selfishness. If you truly care about your grandparents, then you will work to serve them even if it isn't pleasant to you."

Leah looked down at the floor and took a deep breath, "Yes, *mamm*. I'll stay and visit."

"And offer to go back tomorrow," Her mother insisted.

Leah nodded with a sigh and headed out the door where she had a driver waiting in his small silver car.

When she arrived at Grandpa's house, the driver left and promised to return within two hours.

Two hours. Leah shook her head somberly as she made her way to the front door. If this was the way that life was going to be now that she was an adult, she wasn't sure that she liked it one bit!

When she knocked on the door, Grandpa Matthew arrived with something akin to a half-smile on his face.

"Hello, Grandpa!" She announced, "Mom and Dad told me to come by with this for you. Could I maybe serve it up for you and then clean up the dishes?"

"Oh, that would be wonderful."

Leah had dreaded that answer.

"Hello, Leah!" Grandma Bessie greeted her with a sweet smile when she went into her bedroom with some food, "It's so good to see you again, dear. It's been far too long! Just last night I was telling Matthew how I hoped that we could get everyone together soon for a visit. I do miss you all so!"

Leah tried to smile but found it difficult. It was so hard to see her granny lying in a hospital bed, withering away to nothing.

"Leah," Grandpa Matthew took a deep breath, "Is there any chance that you could give me a hand out in the barn for a few minutes once we're finished?"

Leah nodded reluctantly, hoping her lack of enthusiasm didn't show.

As soon as she had cleaned the dishes and put them away, she hurried out to the barn with her grandfather.

Grandpa was preparing for a load of two-hundred newborn calves. His job would be to raise the calves by bottle until they were old enough to eat grass and could be sold to someone else. Preparing for the calves involved constructing individual pens in his large calf barn.

"I certainly am glad to have your help today," Grandpa Matthew announced as he scattered some loose straw in one of the pens, "These jobs sure seem to take longer than ever the older I get."

Leah was starting to wonder how much longer it would be until her driver showed back up.

"Well, who is that?" Grandpa Matthew asked as he looked up from his work.

"It might be my driver," Leah suggested as she hurried to the barn door, surprised to see a buggy pulling into the lane.

Grandpa Matthew stepped out into the sunlight and Leah followed close behind.

"*Ach*, my eyes are failing me," Grandpa muttered as he squinted in the sun, "Who is that?"

Leah didn't have to look close to know, "Its Luke Schmidt."

Just the sight of him left her wanting to run and hide somewhere; seeing him brought up too many bad memories from the night before.

"Hello there Luke!" Grandpa called out as Luke stopped his buggy beside the barn, "How's it going?"

"Doing good, Mr. Eicher," Luke said with a smile as he climbed down from his seat, "How are you?" He turned to Leah and gave a nod, "Good to see you again, Leah."

Leah gave a light nod in return and then headed back inside the barn. From in the doorway, she could hear her grandpa ask, "What brings you out this way, Luke?"

She was just as anxious to hear that answer as her grandfather. It seemed that she was suddenly cursed with seeing Luke everywhere she went, and her sister's teasing made her all the more uneasy.

"I was talking to Leah last night and she told me you had a lot of work going on here at the farm." Luke replied, "Things have slowed down at my place, and I wondered if you could use a hand. I'm thinking about getting into the calf business myself, so the experience would do me good."

Grandpa Matthew was quiet for a minute before he announced, "I don't have any money to pay you and it sure wouldn't be right for you to work for free..."

"The experience would be worth the extra work." Luke persisted.

Leah held her breath. She knew it was wrong of her, but she just hoped Grandpa would turn him away. Quietly, she watched as Grandpa Matthew looked down at his boots and then back up at Luke.

With an out-stretched hand, he announced, "I shouldn't let you, but I sure could use the extra help."

Leah couldn't help but roll her eyes as she watched Luke bumble along behind her grandfather as the old man showed him what needed to be done. Shaking her head slowly, Leah wondered why it couldn't have been Enos to come help on the farm. Goodness knew that with his strength, he would have been far more use than Luke.

"Right now, we're putting together the pens so that we can keep the calves separated," Grandpa explained as he and Luke reached Leah's side, "If you wouldn't mind helping Leah for a few minutes, I really should go check of Bessie."

With that, Grandpa Matthew marched to the house, leaving Leah and Luke alone in the barn.

"I didn't expect to find you here," Luke announced awkwardly as Leah helped him put together a small pen, "Do you help your grandparents often?"

Leah shook her head, "No, I don't."

"Are you feeling better today?"

Somehow, it seemed like Luke had a way of asking the absolute worst thing. Leah nodded curtly, "Yes, I sure am."

"Leah," Luke started to say something when Leah looked up to see a silver car pulling in the drive.

"Oh, my ride's here!" She exclaimed, "I better run in and tell my grandparents goodbye and not keep my driver waiting. See ya, Luke."

That night Leah gathered around the table to eat supper with her family. Her driver had brought her home early enough to help her mom fix canned corn, green beans, fresh rolls, and pork chops.

"I stopped by Grandpa's on my way home from work today," Dad announced as soon as they had finished their silent prayer, "He told me that you were by to see him today, Leah. Thank you for that. I know that your visit truly cheered him up and he said that even Grandma Bessie seems to be doing better after your meal."

Leah's father took a bite of his pork chop and then turned to look at her, "I told him that you could spend a few weeks at his house this summer."

Leah raised her eyebrows in surprise. Staying with her grandparents was not one of her favorite plans and the thought of spending several weeks there almost made her feel sick.

"It's just while his calves are small," Dad was quick to add, "I told him that you could go to his house tomorrow morning and come back here on Friday night."

Leah wanted to protest, but she knew that there was no reason to even try to stand up to her father.

"What about my chores here at home?" She finally managed to ask.

"Amanda can help with those," Her mother replied firmly, "We all have to help each other out when times of trouble happen. Your granny is very sick and your grandpa is tired. If they didn't have so much to do there at the farm, we would simply bring them here to stay, but your grandpa still has his animals. Family is the Lord's gift to us, Leah. Never forget that."

Leah looked down at her plate and tried to swallow her food.

"What do you make of that Schmidt boy helping *daed* out?" Leah's father spoke up, bringing up another topic that she would just as soon avoid, "He certainly seems like a nice young man."

Leah didn't say a word. She could only hope that her work for Grandpa would mostly involve staying in the kitchen and out of Luke Schmidt's sight.

The next morning, Leah's driver picked her up to take her to her grandparents' house. On the way, she stopped at the little Amish store on the outskirts of town to pick up a few things she needed to crochet a blanket for her hope chest.

Her hope chest. For years Leah had gathered small items for her future home and stored them away in the wooden cedar chest her *daed* had made for her. But, at that moment, nothing in life was looking very hopeful.

Stepping into the small store, she headed toward the yarn selection. To her surprise, a young Amish man was looking in the same area, carefully examining a pair of knitting needles. He looked up to acknowledge her presence, and Leah found herself staring into the eyes of Enos Troyer.

"Hello," she managed to mutter, although her voice sounded strange as she tried to form words over the lump in her throat, "How are you, Enos?"

Enos gave a shrug, "Do you know anything about knitting needles?"

"What?"

"My mom wants a pair of size 8 needles. Can you find me some?" Although his voice sounded a bit sharp, Leah was simply excited at the opportunity to help him regardless. She felt almost honored that he would ask for her to lend a hand. Scrambling through the sets of needles, she quickly found the right size and handed it to him.

"Your mom must be good at knitting," she said the first thing that came to mind, "I'm looking for yarn to make a throw. Which color do you think would be best?"

Enos grunted and announced, "I'm late for work." Without so much as a thank you, he hurried to pay for his items and be on his way.

He was probably truly in a hurry, Leah tried to console herself as she gathered her yarn and started toward the front of the store. But, no matter what Leah told herself, his behavior hurt. It made her feel bad that Enos paid her no mind at all. What was wrong with him? But what grated on her mind the most was the worry that something might be wrong with her.

Standing so close to him had put her heart in a flutter. As she reached to pass him the pair of knitting needles, their hands had met and Leah was sure that she felt a tingle run up her arm. How could he not notice?

Surely what Leah was feeling had to be true love. Enos just hadn't gotten around to realizing it but, given time, he would and together they could have a love that would blossom into a lifelong romance. Leah just couldn't give up!

Chapter Four

Leah discovered that most of her chores around Grandpa Matthew's house were simple and relatively easy. He left her in the house with Grandma Bessie so he and Luke could do the barn work. Leah's responsibilities included dusting the house, scrubbing the floors, and keeping the laundry clean.

"It sure is good to see someone so young and happy in my house," Grandma Bessie announced when Leah went in to check on her, "It's been a long time since anyone has been that lively around here! How old are you now, dear? Since I've been sick, I haven't been able to keep up at all."

Leah smiled as she lifted a dust cloth to wipe off the bed frame, "I just turned sixteen."

"*Ach*, sixteen," Grandma smiled at the thought of it, "I was sixteen when I first met your grandpa at a young peoples' gathering. I'll never forget that day, because he accidentally spilled a glass of milk down the front of my good dress." Grandma Bessie laughed and shook her head, "I certainly never thought he'd be the man I'd marry...strangle, perhaps, but never marry." Grandma was silent for a moment and then finally broke the still with a question, "Have any young men caught your eye?"

Leah wasn't sure how much she wanted to reveal to her grandmother, but slowly nodded "yes".

Grandma leaned back against her pillow and took a deep breath, wincing as a wave of pain came over her.

"Tell me about him?" She asked softly.

"Well," Leah smiled just at the thought of Enos, "He's tall and handsome, Grandma, and ever so strong! Whenever I'm around him, my stomach turns to butterflies and I get so incredibly nervous. I feel like, if we were to ever touch, fireworks would surely start to shoot off!"

Grandma Bessie smiled, "Ah, fireworks and butterflies..." her voice trailed off and Leah thought she was about to go to sleep when she opened her eyes again and announced, "Relationships aren't all fireworks and butterflies, Leah. Those are nice, but they never last for the long run. Real love is about commitment...and prayer...and a lot of forgiveness."

Leah raised an eyebrow. A lot Grandma Bessie knew about love. As far as Leah knew, she and Grandpa had never been more than simply roommates. From the time that Leah was a little girl, their relationship had been obviously strained and it never seemed to get any better with time. Sure, Grandpa spent time taking good care of his wife and was obviously concerned about her, but there was definitely something lack.

No, Leah wouldn't be paying too much attention to Grandma Bessie. Things turned out a bit better in the romance books she loved to read, so she would be happy to keep her butterflies and fireworks!

Leah spent most of the first morning catching up on the household chores that Grandpa Matthew had let go for far too long. The laundry alone seemed endless and there were so many dishes in the sink, it looked like he'd had the entire community over for dinner.

At lunch, Grandpa and Luke came in from the calf barn to enjoy Leah's meal of potato salad, fried chicken, and fresh rolls.

"We've accomplished a lot this morning," Grandpa announced as he started loading his plate down with potato salad, "With Luke's help, I've been able to get much more done than I could have ever hoped to finish by myself...which is a good thing since our calves are supposed to be delivered tomorrow."

Luke shook his head with embarrassment, "I can hardly thank you enough for the chance to work with you."

Grandpa Matthew didn't say a word, but Leah could tell that he wasn't buying Luke's story. Leah knew that she certainly didn't either. Lying obviously wasn't one of Luke's finest skills. She remembered him asking about her grandparents at the young peoples' get-together and was certain that all his help was simply an attempt to relieve some of the load off of her granddad.

Despite the fact that he had played a part in her awful sixteenth birthday, Luke was not a bad person. Honestly, Leah had only good memories of the time they spent together when she was helping out with his baby brothers. But Luke Schmidt would never be more than a mere acquaintance – Leah would make sure of that!

Suddenly, Leah realized that she was staring straight at Luke when his eyes looked up and met hers. She wondered how long she had been looking at him and if anyone else had noticed.

"That Luke Schmidt is a good worker!" Grandpa Matthew commented as he sat down in his rocking chair with a groan.

Darkness was beginning to close in, and Leah was sitting nearby with her crocheting in hand. Her afghan was well underway, leaving Leah to only hope that the blue color she chose would be something Enos would like.

Just hearing more about Luke made Leah want to leave them room. Every time someone mentioned him, it felt like they were trying to push him in her direction. Why couldn't everyone just leave her alone?

She sincerely hoped that Grandpa hadn't noticed her staring at him during the meal that afternoon.

"When is he coming back?" She asked with a sigh.

"*Ach*, poor boy is coming back in the morning." Grandpa replied with a laugh, "He wants to be here to help when the calves are unloaded and help me get them settled in. Seems he wants to lend a hand around here for a few weeks until I get the calves raised up a bit and make sure they are all healthy." Grandpa shook his head with a sad smile, "Boys like that are hard to find."

Leah bit her tongue and looked down at her work. Certainly, it was nice of Luke to be helping out so much and it would be hard to find someone so willing to lend a hand, but he was still no match for Enos Troyer. Enos was the type of man Leah wanted to marry; Luke was simply the kind she was glad to know.

The next morning, Luke arrived at the house as Leah was washing off the breakfast dishes.

"I didn't miss the calves, did I?"

Leah shook her head, "No, Grandpa is with Grandma Bessie back in the bedroom."

"How is she doing?" Luke asked as he grabbed the dishrag and reached to dry some of the newly washed dishes.

"She had a rough night," Leah said with a sigh as she thought about hearing her grandfather pace the floor even from her bedroom upstairs, the lowered her voice to add, "I think Grandpa is worried she won't make it through the summer."

Luke nodded his head, "Seems like it weights on him all the time."

"You don't have to do that," Leah interrupted, pointing a soapy finger toward the dish that he was drying, "I can take care of the dishes myself."

Luke smirked and gave a shrug, "Drying dishes was my job growing up. I tend to think of myself as a bit of an expert."

"Doesn't your Mamm miss your "expert" help at home?" Leah had been wondering how Luke managed to leave his own family to come work with her grandfather.

"Well," Luke looked down at the dish he was drying, "I think they understand. I still get all my morning chores done at home before I come here, then I finish my other chores with my brothers before bed. This is only for a few weeks; everybody knows that. I just want your grandpa to have a good chance with this load of calves. Maybe once he gets this load raised up and sold, he can take a break for the winter."

Luke's voice trailed off as they head footsteps headed their direction. Grandpa Matthew came into the kitchen, dressed and ready for the day of work ahead of him. His mouth was drawn into a frown and worry seemed to cloud his entire face.

"*Gut* morning, sir," Luke called out as Grandpa Matthew came to his side, "Are you ready for a day of work?"

Grandpa nodded his head, "*Jah*, we'd better get out to the barn and start preparing for those calves – the truck should be here within the next hour."

Before they could head out the door, Grandpa turned to look at Leah and said, "Keep a close eye on your grandma today. She had a very rough night."

Leah scrubbed the last bit of scrambled egg off of the cast-iron skillet and then wiped her wet hands on her apron.

Having Luke there was truly a blessing. She wasn't sure how Grandpa Matthew could do all the work by himself. Although Leah hated the extra work and being away from home, she had to admit that her parents had been wise to send her to stay with her grandparents.

She could hear her grandmother let out a moan in the other room, and Leah hurried to go check on her.

Grandma Bessie finally drifted off to sleep and Leah was free to do regular housework. She spent the morning scrubbing the kitchen floor and cleaning out the cabinets. Since grandma had been sick so long, Grandpa Matthew had gotten in the habit of simply throwing pots and pans in any way he could, leaving Leah quite a mess.

By the time the trailer full of calves arrived, Leah was about to pull her hair out in frustration from her work. Deciding to take a quick break, she hurried out to the yard to watch the trailer unload.

There was something about calves that tugged at Leah's heartstrings. Even as a little girl, she had loved to go out to the barn and help her *daed* in the barn. She secretly hoped that Grandpa Matthew would give her the chance to lend a hand now.

From the front porch, Leah watched as the trailer backed up to the barn and the calves were unloaded into their pens. Even from a distance, she could hear the familiar "mooing" of baby calves and could smell the fresh scent of hay wafting from the barn.

When the calves were finally all unloaded, the trailer door was slammed shut, and the truck rolled away. Leah watched as the big tires turned around and around, leading the truck down her grandparents' driveway and to its next location.

"Don't you wanna come see the calves?"

Leah jumped when she heard a voice beside her, suddenly realizing that Luke had come to her side while she was lost in thought.

"Your granddad and I have them all in pens. They're pretty cute!"

Leah couldn't help but smile at Luke's enthusiasm. She nodded her head and followed him out to the barn.

"There's two-hundred and fifty-five calves," Luke informed her as he opened the barn door and led her inside.

The dark barn was filled with pens of calves. Grandpa was hurrying to set up bottles for each of them to drink out of, giving them the nutrition they needed for a good start.

"What do ya think, Leah?" Grandpa Matthew called out as he set another bottle in place.

"They're adorable!" Leah exclaimed as she reached out to pet one of the little creatures on its soft, wet nose.

"I have a good feeling about this bunch of calves," Grandpa announced as he came to stand by her side, wiping his hands on the legs of his black pants, "These are the healthiest calves we've had yet. With you and Luke helping, I think we can get the whole bunch grown up and free of sickness."

Leah hoped that her Grandpa was right, but realized that his enthusiasm was mostly just wishful thinking. With all of Grandma Bessie's recent bills, he would need every penny he could make from these calves. He couldn't afford to lose even one of them.

Leah and Luke gave each other knowing looks. Somehow, it felt good to have Luke there with her; it made Leah feel like she had someone on her team. Together, she hoped that they could get Grandpa through this difficult time in his life.

Chapter Five

Time at Grandpa's house was strange. In some ways, it felt like each hour flew by since Leah had so much work to keep her busy; on the other hand, time also seemed to drag. Every day, she found herself exhausted and overwhelmed by the monotony of taking care of Grandpa Bessie, cooking, cleaning, and helping with the calves.

By Thursday, it felt like Leah had been gone from home for a month. She was cleaning away the lunch dishes when Luke took a deep breath and announced, "I'm going to make a run into town to pick up some extra boards to repair that place in the barn."

Grandpa Matthew nodded his head and took a drink of his iced tea, "Sounds like a good plan. Since most of the work is done, I think I'm going to sit with Bessie for a while."

Luke stood up from his place at the table, the feet of his chair legs scraping across the hardwood floor as he found his feet. Grabbing a dirty plate off the table, Luke started helping Leah clean up the mess.

Something about Luke seemed unusual. Rather than being ready to go back to work as he was every afternoon, he lingered in the kitchen at the sink, glancing out the window and then down at the floor.

"Leah," he finally found his voice, "Would you want to come into town with me?"

The words surprised Leah so much that she almost dropped the plate she was washing on the floor. Leah wasn't sure that she was ready to be seen out and about with Luke Schmidt but, considering how desperately she needed a break from the monotony of work, the idea of a trip with anyone was almost worth it.

"Sure," she finally announced, "I need a few things anyway...if that's okay with Grandpa."

Glancing at Grandpa Matthew, she saw him give a happy smirk. *Ach*, she could hardly stand what he probably thought. Grandpa was completely sold on Luke and Leah was certain he had hopes that Luke would someday be an in-law. That was a dream Leah wasn't going to make come true!

"Do ya mind, Grandpa?" She already knew the answer before the words escaped her lips.

Grandpa shrugged his shoulders, "Of course not. Just remember to pick up some more saltine crackers for the coffee soup!"

Leah hurried to wash the few dishes from dinner and, with Luke's help, the job was done quickly enough. Within a half hour, they were both situated in Luke's buggy and on their way to town.

"This shouldn't take me too long," Luke told her as he guided his horse down the road, "I just need to stop by the lumber store and get a couple of things."

"It won't take me long either," Leah returned, "I just need a few things from the grocery. I'm afraid Grandpa Matthew hasn't been the best at keeping the house stocked with food."

Luke laughed and shrugged his shoulders, "I know from shopping with my *mamm* that a trip to the grocery store can never be quick!" Leah couldn't help but laugh along at Luke's accurate statement. He was quiet for a moment and then asked, "*Ach*, Leah, how long has your granny been sick now?"

The cheerful mood was suddenly gone as Leah found herself weighed down by the sorrow of her grandparents' situation. She took a deep breath and looked out across the fields of a nearby farm, "Almost a year. She was taking treatment, but it just didn't seem to help. I think everybody's about given up hope now. Seems like we're all just waiting on the worse to happen now. Just thinking about Granny Bessie dying seems so sad – it makes me hate staying there."

Neither of them spoke. Leah found herself struggling not to cry as she thought about all the good times she had with her grandmother before the cancer took its toll. As a little girl, she could remember spending afternoons with Granny Bessie, cutting out paper dolls and baking apple pies together. The thought that Granny would never again be able to do those things broke her heart. Sometimes Leah felt almost guilty that she didn't want to be around her grandparents, but seeing Granny in such bad shape was more than she could hardly stand.

"Luke," she finally managed to say, "Do you think I'm a terrible person?"

Luke laughed and looked at her in surprise, "What do you mean?"

"For saying I hate staying with my grandparents. Do you think that makes me an awful person?"

Luke was silent for a moment, making Leah wonder if he didn't want to answer her question.

"Of course not, Leah," he said gently, "No one would enjoy seeing their granny suffer, but the fact that you go on and help your grandparents anyway...that shows that you really love them."

Leah felt like she might cry. Somehow, Luke knew exactly how to ease her fears. She didn't know why his approval meant so much to her, but hearing him say that she wasn't an awful person did something good for her and lifted a weight off her chest.

They rode in silence for several minutes, listening to the birds whistle in the trees overhead and feeling the gentle breeze in their faces.

"What do you like to do for fun?" Leah asked, trying to take the conversation in a new direction. She didn't know why she was even trying to talk to Luke; she couldn't decide if her questions were more about making small talk or about truly learning who Luke Schmidt was.

Luke thought for a moment and then smiled, "I like taking care of animals....and planting things in the garden. I like watching the little vegetable sprouts come up out of the dirt. There's something about it that's just..." Luke took a deep breath, "Magical, I guess."

Leah glanced at the young man sitting beside her. His round face had turned a shade of red and he was staring straight ahead at the road. She almost laughed, but held it in, realizing that Luke wasn't one to share things like that very often. Laughing at his humiliation would surely hurt him deeply.

"I like to read," she announced, hurrying to change the subject.

"Ick," Luke shook his head, "I never was good at reading. I never was good at school, really. My *daed* worried himself silly that I wouldn't get out of school until I was twenty-five."

They both laughed and Leah said, "I can't imagine not reading. It's such an escape...it's a way to get to really live life. You can experience all kinds of exciting things, even when life is dull and boring."

Luke shrugged his shoulders, "I guess I've always been happy with dull and boring."

"Don't you ever want anything exciting? Don't you dream about the future?"

Leah's question made Luke smile, "Oh, sure. I plan to work and save back enough money to buy myself a big farm."

A farm. Leah fought the urge to roll her eyes. Of course, every Amish man wanted a farm of his own. It wasn't much of a dream.

"What will you do on your farm?" She forced herself to ask.

"Oh, I just want to raise things...you know, cows, sheep, chickens, corn, grain,..."

"I think I get the idea," Leah smiled as she interrupted him, "If it's possible, you want it."

Luke chuckled and nodded, "I guess that's about right. Other than that, I just want a life where I can take care of my family and raise my children to care about other people and to care about God."

Suddenly, the conversation seemed too serious. Leah certainly didn't like to think of herself married to Luke, but surprisingly enough, the idea of him being married to someone else seemed almost worse!

Leah looked down at her hands and tried to imagine what Luke's wife would be like. The days of friendship between Leah and Luke would be over then; of course, it wouldn't matter at that point...Leah would already be Mrs. Enos Troyer and Luke would be no more than a memory. By then, Luke would be nothing to her.

Ach, Leah! She scolded herself, *What are you thinking? Luke isn't anything to you now!*

True to his word, Luke was out of the lumber store in a matter of minutes, carrying some wooden boards to repair some damage in her grandpa's barn wall. When Leah showed him her long list of grocery items, he agreed to go in and help her find what she needed.

"Better than sitting out here alone," he said with a smirk as he tied the horse's reigns to a hitching post.

Leah was actually glad to have someone with her. The store was frequented by Amish from her community, but the majority of the customers and all of the workers were English. Leah had very little experience shopping alone among so many strangers, and having a friend by her side gave her some confidence.

To Leah's surprise, they weren't the only Amish in the grocery store. As soon as they stepped into the market, Leah spotted a group of teenage boys wandering down the potato chip aisle. Her heart instantly gave a leap as she recognized one of the taller young men as Enos Troyer.

Leah felt like she might faint as her stomach filled with butterflies.

"What are we here for first?" Luke asked, obviously not having noticed the other boys.

Leah pulled the list out of her dress pocket. Her hands were trembling so much that she could hardly unfold the paper, and she felt completely disoriented as she tried to read the items she had written down.

"We need a bag of flour," she managed to mutter, "I'd like one of those big bags."

Luke gave a smile, "I hope this is a sign that you're about ready to make some cookies!"

Leah tried to laugh but could hardly make a sound. *Ach*, how was it possible for her to feel so completely unlike herself? If this wasn't love, she didn't know what could be!

As they started down the aisle with the baking supplies, Leah and Luke were met head-on by Enos and the three other boys he had with him.

Leah looked down at her shoes, suddenly more awkward than she could begin to say.

"Hello," Luke greeted them, his voice sounding somewhat strained and a bit unfriendly.

The other Amish boys nodded, some of them saying a quick "hey" before they went on down the aisle.

"Who was that?" Leah overheard one of the boys ask.

"Fatty Luke Schmidt," She heard Enos' voice sneer, "I don't know who that girl was. I hope we can get out with our groceries before he buys up all the food."

Leah glanced at Luke who was bending over to grab a bag of flour. She couldn't tell if he head heard Enos' comment, but had a hard time believing that he didn't.

She felt bad for him, but she felt even worse for herself. How was she ever supposed to have a hope of catching Enos Troyer if she was simply known as the girl who hung out with "Fatty" Luke Schmidt? It didn't seem like a very promising start to a romantic relationship.

Maybe it was time for Leah to start distancing herself from Luke. No matter what, she wouldn't be accepting any more rides from him any time soon.

Despite her disappointing encounter with Enos, Leah had a pleasant ride back to her grandparents' house. She and Luke shared a bag of potato chips and some soda. Luke told her about some of the funny things that the calves had done and about his plans to name some of his favorites.

When they arrived at Grandpa Matthew's it was mid-afternoon.

"I guess I'd better help your grandpa with the feeding and then get back home," Luke announced, "My *daed* needs me to do some work on the chicken house."

"Thanks for the ride to town," Leah said as Luke helped her carry the groceries into the house, "We desperately needed these supplies. I want to bake enough bread to keep Grandpa going over the weekend while I'm back at home with my parents."

"Would you want a ride home Friday night?" For some reason, Luke's question surprised Leah. She had planned all week to hire a driver to take her back to her parents' house.

She stood on the porch in indecision, trying to decide on an answer.

"That would actually be nice," she told him.

Leah could hardly believe the words that had just come out of her own mouth. What was she thinking? She had just decided that it was time to distance herself from Luke and here she went throwing herself in his path again!

It was dark and, once again, Matthew found himself unable to sleep. This seemed to be the way that his life went these days. Night after night he would find himself wide awake, staring up at the dark ceiling, listening to his wife's shallow breaths. When he did fall asleep, Matthew was plagued by horrible nightmares.

He could never forgive himself for the things that he had done wrong.

Sitting up in bed, he studied his wife's sleeping form.

"Dear Lord," he started to pray, but found that no more words would come. He wanted so much to tear down the division that stood between him and his creator. Matthew wanted to let the words come naturally, to flow from his heart, but it seemed that was not to be. Too much guilt stood between him and God, and Matthew found himself unable to even formulate adequate words for a prayer.

Just like his relationship with Bessie had been destroyed, it seemed that his relationship with God was a thing of the past as well. At times like this, Matthew wished that he and his wife could trade places. He so wished that he could simply be done with this life while she went on to enjoy some good years with just their family....years that could be free from the cloud he had brought over their marriage.

"Please," he managed to whisper, "Let my wife recover. I don't care what you do to me, but please get her past this."

Chapter Six

The ride home on Friday afternoon was a pure delight. Not only was Leah excited to be going back to stay with her family, but the off-weekend without church assured her that she would get some much-needed rest.

Despite the fact that Luke was still going to give her grandpa some minimal help with the calves over the weekend, he was also in good spirits. The entire trip home, he entertained Leah with funny stories about his little brothers and tales of their shenanigans.

"Oh," Leah tried to recover from laughing as he finished a story about one of his brothers getting stuck on the roof of the house, "You must enjoy your family a lot."

Luke nodded his head, "Sure do. I don't know what I'd do without them."

They were both silent. Leah found herself admiring the fact that he could honestly appreciate his family and find joy in living with them. So many young men treated their families like little more than a nuisance and were more than ready to break free and be out on their own.

"Would you like to come to my house tomorrow afternoon?" Luke asked, his uncertainty showing in his voice, "We're going to be having a cookout on my dad's new grill."

Leah glanced at Luke and watched him working his hands together nervously around the reigns to the horses. He was scared silly. Leah found herself almost feeling sorry for him, but his actions made her uncomfortable. Was this supposed to be a date?

"I'm supposed to be helping him with the hamburgers, so I can't guarantee that the food will be too good," he added.

"I'm sure the food will be good," Leah replied with a smile, "I trust your cooking skills."

Luke looked at her out of the corner of his eye, "So, you think you might want to come? I could pick you up around noon, if ya want."

Go to Luke's house for a cookout? What sense would that make? There was no reason to lead the poor boy on to believe that he had any hope. After all, Leah had her cap set for Enos Troyer.

"Well," she answered slowly, "after spending so much time with your mom after the twins were born, it would be *gut* to see her again. Sure, I guess I can come."

Leah couldn't help but notice the broad smile that spread across Luke's face. She couldn't believe that she had let herself be talked into visiting Luke's family. Certainly, she had made it sound like she simply wanted to spend time with his *mamm*, but the truth of the matter was that Leah had been more anxious to just spend extra time around Luke. After being with him all week at her grandparents' home, she hated not seeing him over the weekend. What was wrong with her? She couldn't figure it out herself.

Luke was certainly a dear friend, but Leah was starting to wonder if she wasn't letting herself grow a little too fond of him. Luke had no place in Leah's life. She had to remember that.

The next afternoon, after Leah endured a lot of teasing from Amanda, Luke picked her up and gave her a ride to his family's large white farm house.

"*Ach*, Leah, it certainly is good to have you here!" Mrs. Schmidt greeted her with a hug as she invited her into their kitchen, "I've missed you a lot! I have to admit that your company spoiled me last summer."

Luke was the oldest of seven boys and the family had no girls. Leah remembered Mrs. Schmidt saying that she wished she had a little girl but, so far, the Lord had seen fit to only bless them with rough boys.

"It's good to see you again, too." Leah replied with a smile. Although she felt uncomfortable going to Luke's house in what appeared to be a date, there was something about his family that always made her feel at home.

"When Luke invited me to come today, I couldn't resist seeing you," Leah threw in quickly, hoping that Luke's *mamm* wouldn't get any ideas about their friendship. The last thing Leah wanted to do was lead this family to hope for a relationship that would never develop.

Mrs. Schmidt seemed to pay no attention to her comment, and instead led her to the kitchen where she set Leah to work making fresh hamburger patties, cutting potatoes into French fries, and slicing homegrown tomatoes.

Standing by the pump sink, Leah could watch Luke, his *daed*, and the six other boys out on the back porch. While Mr. Schmidt got the grill ready, Luke reached down and picked up his twin brothers, holding one under each arm. The little boys laughed as he sailed them through the air like they were traveling in one of the *Englisher's* fancy airplanes.

He will make a gut dad someday, Leah thought to herself as she shaped a handful of hamburger into a patty.

"Leah, are ya hearing a word I'm saying?"

Leah snapped to attention when she realized that Mrs. Schmidt had been talking to her. She felt her face grow red as she slowly shook her head.

"I'm sorry, Mrs. Schmidt, I was somewhere else. Worrying about my Grandma, I suppose." Leah felt bad lying, but she couldn't let anyone know that she had truly been studying Luke.

Mrs. Schmidt nodded gently and went on to ask about Granny Bessie, obviously buying into the fib that Leah had told.

Just as Leah had expected, the food was delicious. Together, the family gathered around an outdoor picnic table and enjoyed French fries, hamburgers, and homemade potato chips. They laughed together and talked about things that were happening in the community.

Leah found herself feeling at peace and, amazingly enough, hardly wanted to leave.

Before she went home that night, she had already agreed to let Luke drive her to her grandparents' house the next week.

Leah wasn't even sure how it happened but, suddenly, it seemed that she and Luke had developed a habit of spending time together. Whether they were working on her granddad's farm, laughing together over lunch, cleaning up the dishes as a team, or going to events, Leah didn't seem to go a day without seeing Luke.

The year before, she felt as if she and Luke had developed a decent friendship traveling back and forth from his house after she helped care for his twin brothers, but this was much more.

Leah found herself actually looking forward to seeing Luke every morning and, on days when he was late getting there, she was almost disappointed.

Time actually started to go faster and Leah was beginning to adjust to life at her grandparents' house.

The next weekend, Luke drove her home on his buggy and they spent the entire ride laughing together over things that had happened during the week.

When they pulled into her parents' driveway, Leah reached for her black bag, anxious to go into the house and enjoy some time with her family. She also wanted to get out of Luke's buggy before Amanda had more ammunition to tease her. Before she could get down, Luke stopped her.

"Leah," he was quiet for a minute before he asked, "Are you planning to stay after church Sunday? Or will you just go to the young peoples' gathering after?"

Leah shrugged her shoulders uncertainly, "I figured I might as well just go home. Waiting gets pretty boring pretty fast."

Luke laughed, "I'd imagine so. I was just going to say, if ya want a ride, I'd be glad to pick you up and then take you home after."

Leah found herself caught in indecision. As much fun as she had with Luke that day, she still thought often about the words she had overheard Enos say in the grocery store. If she was seen out with "Fatty" Luke too often, she was likely to ruin her chances with Enos entirely.

"Well," she reached up to readjust her bonnet, "I suppose it would be better than hiring a driver."

Although she realized that her reply had been less than enthusiastic and almost insulting, Luke's face broke out into a sincere smile.

"All right, then!" He exclaimed, "I'll pick ya up at your house on Sunday afternoon. Would around five-thirty suit you?"

Leah gave a disinterested shrug, "Sounds good to me."

When Sunday night finally came, Leah found herself full of jitters. It was only her second young peoples' gathering but she was determined to make it a good one. Each minute that passed, she was more anxious than ever to get to see Enos Troyer.

Maybe tonight would be the night that he would talk to her!

Leah had a nice ride to the gathering with Luke, although she found it hard to pay any attention to him when she was so anxious to get on to the excitement. She was determined that, no matter what, she would get to speak to Enos and try her best to win his heart.

They arrived at the gathering late and the events were already well underway. Stepping into the barn, Leah looked for Enos and found him playing corn-hole with some of the other boys.

Gathering her determination, Leah took a deep breath and tried to remember all the things she had hoped to say.

"Thanks for the ride, Luke." She announced dryly when she realized that her traveling companion seemed intent on staying by her side, "I'll see you around." With that, she quickly moved away from Luke and started toward Enos.

Standing in the sidelines with some of the other girls, Leah made small talk and watched Enos while he played the game.

He was so strong and athletic! Leah couldn't help but marvel at the way that he threw the beanbags and always made the target.

No surprise to anyone, Enos won the game.

Raising his arms in the air, Enos announced, "Say hello to the champion!"

When someone suggested he play another round, Enos shook his head and wiped some sweat from his forehead, "No, I've got to get a drink."

Leah was quick to follow him to the snack table, hurrying to keep up with his long strides.

"You are such a good player!" Leah announced, hoping that Enos could hear her over the noise of the other young folk, "I've never seen anyone any better at corn-hole."

Enos reached out to a pitcher of lemonade and poured it into a glass. "You haven't seen it, because there is no one better," He announced as he lifted the drink to his mouth.

"I saw you in the grocery store the other day," Leah wished that she could think of something sensible to say, but it felt like she was floundering with every word that escaped her mouth.

Enos raised an eyebrow, "I don't remember."

Leah tried to laugh but it came out sounding fake even to her own ears, "Well, I just thought I'd introduce myself. I'm Leah Eicher. I go to church with you every Sunday."

Enos was staring right at her now, but his face certainly was not friendly; instead, Enos examined her like one might a rather disgusting worm.

"I don't mean to be rude," he announced, his voice full of disdain, "but I need to get back to my game."

"Maybe we can talk later tonight..." Leah started to say but Enos interrupted her.

"Listen, little girl, I'm very busy. I don't have time to talk."

With that, Enos marched away, leaving Leah all alone.

If she had felt bad at the last gathering, this was much worse. Leah felt like she might throw up. She was filled with a mixture of both humiliation and heartbreak. No matter what she said or did, Enos paid no attention to her at all.

Leah found a hay bale in the corner of the barn and sat alone in the darkness. She had no desire to talk to anyone. She just wanted to be hidden from view, alone with her aching heart.

Closing her eyes, Leah fought back the tears. What was wrong with her? Why didn't Enos like her? Was it because she wasn't as pretty as some of the other girls? Was it because she was simply too young for him? Was it that she had nothing worthwhile to say?

Leah mentally went over the things that she had said to him, wondering what she could have done differently, what she could have said that would have made him pay attention to her.

"Leah," she heard a gentle and familiar voice speak her name. She didn't have to look up to realize that it was Luke.

"Leah," he repeated, "Are you all right? Are you having any fun at all?"

Leah shook her head, "No, I'm not. I want to go home."

Luke didn't put up a fight at all; instead, he simply said, "I'll go get the buggy."

The ride home started with silence. Leah couldn't force herself to start to talk. The mere idea of opening her mouth made her feel like she would burst into tears. It seemed that Luke also knew that talking wasn't worth even trying.

Finally, Luke cleared his throat, breaking the thick silence.

"Leah," Luke was quiet for so long, Leah wondered if he was going to finish what he had started, "I know you always want to talk to Enos Troyer...and so far, you haven't had much luck."

Leah felt her face growing warm and she was almost overcome by an urge to slap her friend across the mouth. How did he know that? Had he been spying on her?

"What do you know about anything?" Leah snapped, crossing her arms across her chest and jutting out her lower jaw.

"You're too good for him, Leah," Luke plowed ahead, "I've spent time with Enos and I know what he's like. There are a lot of nice boys in our community – lots nicer than Enos. I'm not asking you to like me, but I wish you would choose somebody better than him."

"It's a good thing you're not asking me to like you," Leah announced sharply, "because I certainly don't and I never will. Now, I'd appreciate it if you said nothing more about this subject and just get me home as soon as possible."

As soon as the words were out of her mouth, Leah regretted them. She felt guilty for what she'd said, but wasn't sure how to make things right. Luke didn't say another word; instead, he simply followed her command and took her back to her house.

Chapter Seven

Despite Leah's harsh comments, by Monday morning Luke acted as if the entire scene had never happened. Leah found herself wondering if she should apologize, but instead chose to let the entire incident simply pass by. Perhaps Luke realized that he had been in the wrong to even mention it. After all, Leah's life was none of his business and he had no right to say anything about the way that she chose to live it.

Luke continued to take Leah back and forth to her home on the weekends and, to Leah's surprise, even asked to take her to more young peoples' meetings.

Leah had not given up on Enos but realized that, until he stepped forward and saw that she was the perfect girl for him, she would enjoy her time with Luke. Luke was a good friend and as close as a brother. The rides he gave Leah not only offered her some entertainment and good company, but also saved her the money she would have to pay a driver. Yes, until things changed with Enos, she would take Luke up on his offers.

One morning, Leah and Luke had a hard day of work cleaning out the barn. Grandpa was tired from a long night up with Grandma Bessie, so he stayed inside while they cleaned out all the dirty stalls and put down fresh bedding.

Leah had to admit that Luke made the distasteful chore fun as he joked about what the calves must think of their work and shared stories about his favorite jobs as a boy.

At noon, their job was finished and Grandpa called them inside for a meal of leftover baked chicken and noodles.

"Better get back out there and see about mending one of the pens," Luke announced as he finished off his glass of tea.

"Why don't you two take a break?" Grandpa Matthew asked as he reached out to help put away a pile of clean plates, "You're both worn out. Here," Reaching in his pocket, he pulled out his wallet and began to scramble for some change, "Run to town and pick us up a pizza, will ya? It would make a nice supper."

Luke shifted his weight from one foot to the other, "Leah, what do you say?"

Leah resented what she took as her grandpa's attempts at matchmaking, but she quickly nodded her head, "I guess I could go along. Some fresh air might do me good."

Hurrying to put away the last of the dishes, Leah found herself actually enjoying the thought of some time alone with Luke.

Watching the young couple pull out of his driveway, Matthew took a deep breath and shook his head. The entire situation between those two puzzled him.

He knew that Leah liked Luke. He could tell whenever they were together. In fact, sometimes it seemed that she almost tried to seek him out. There were plenty of times when she trailed out to the barn to deliver to ask questions that could certainly wait, and he'd noticed her sneaking plenty of glances in Luke's direction. Why exactly she fought so hard to act like she didn't care was beyond Matthew's understanding. It was almost as if she didn't want to care about Luke...or even tolerate him, for that matter.

Back in the times long past, he would have gone to Bessie and talked over these questions with her. She had always had a way of sorting things out and explaining situations from a different perspective. But the days of sharing anything was long past.

Matthew realized that he had destroyed that chance forty years ago when he shut the door on his heart and left her on the outside. It was too late to try to change things now. The secrets that stood between him and Bessie were too big to ever hope to get past with something as trivial as the romantic interests of their sixteen-year-old granddaughter.

Leah had a fantastic time in town with Luke, and she could see that she wasn't the only one. She had never seen him smile more or talk as much. It seemed that they had grown so comfortable with one another that they could share anything.

They got the pizza and then stopped by the ice cream shop to get a delicious snack. Sitting on one of the outdoor picnic tables, they enjoyed watching butterflies and talking about their lives.

"I helped to build these picnic tables," Luke announced as he tapped the top of one of the pieces of wooden furniture.

Leah looked at him in surprise, "Really?"

"Yeah. Up until this summer, I was working on a construction crew with my dad. I've been trying to save back a little bit of money..."

"For your farm?" Leah asked before he could finish.

Luke nodded, "Of course. Every penny I make is for my farm. That's one of my biggest dreams."

Leah leaned her arm against the top of the table, silently admiring the craftsmanship, "What are you other dreams?"

Luke laughed and looked across the parking lot, "Hmmm...not fair. I've told you too much about me. It's time for me to hear some things about you."

"*Ach*, I don't know." Leah shrugged, trying to decide how much to tell. Honestly, apart from Enos Troyer, it was hard to remember having any dreams at all.

"Come on," Luke gave her a gentle nudge with his elbow, "I've told you some of my dreams. It's not right for me to know nothing about what you want out of life."

Suddenly, Leah felt completely unsure of herself and terribly awkward.

"I'm not even sure, Luke," she muttered as she wiped up some ice cream with her napkin, "Sometimes I think I have everything figured out, but other times, I'm just not certain at all. It feels like I make big plans and then they fall apart."

Sneaking a glance at Luke, she saw that he didn't look disgusted but instead understanding.

"You know, I think we're all like that sometimes. I guess the best we can do is simply try to follow God's plan and figure that, when things fall apart, He must have something better in mind."

Luke's words were true, but Leah wasn't sure how to take them. She had made up her mind that Enos was the man for her – she had spent so much time praying that he would be her husband, the idea that God might have something better seemed impossible. Sadly, if things didn't change soon, Leah was afraid that she would give up hope completely. Although she had now attended several get-togethers for the young folk, Enos continued to give her the cold shoulder. Could it be God's plan that they not be together?

Suddenly, Leah's ice cream tasted bitter in her mouth and she was glad when Luke suggested they head back to her grandparents' house.

"I had a good time this afternoon," Luke announced as he pulled the wagon into her grandparents' driveway after they returned from their trip to town, "The best time I've had in a while."

"*Ach*," Leah shook her head, "Does ice cream really make you that happy?"

Luke laughed and then grew a bit more serious, "No, but you do."

In all their time together, Luke had never said anything so sweet. Leah always knew she was special to her friend, but hearing him say it brought on a round of strange emotions. Suddenly, Leah felt more awkward than she had in her entire life. She began to wonder if she would even be able to open her mouth and say anything at all. She wasn't even sure what she wanted to say.

Leah found herself fighting the urge to say things that would change the course of her life. She wanted to just open her heart and announce that she'd had fun too. She wanted to admit that spending time with Luke was better than spending time with anyone else she knew. But instead, she looked away and haughtily announced, "It was a relief to go anywhere with anyone. I was ready to get away and see someone other than Grandpa and Grandma."

Luke didn't say another word, and Leah found herself almost feeling guilty.

As soon as they pulled into the barnyard, Grandpa Matthew came hurrying out of the barn, obviously anxious to talk to them.

"We brought the pizza," Luke announced, lifting up the bags of frozen pizza as he pulled his horse to a stop.

"*Ach*, Luke, no time for that!" Grandpa exclaimed, "One of the calves is sick. Bad sick. I need your help. We've got to give her some shots."

Leah let out a moan. She knew that Grandpa was facing so many medical bills. He had hoped that every calf would make it so that he would be able to get the best return on his investment. Even the death of one calf meant that he would lose out on hundreds of much-needed dollars. She could only hope that Grandpa and Luke would be able to do something to save the little creature's life.

All afternoon Luke and Grandpa Matthew stayed out in the barn, working hard to try to nurse the calf back to health. Leah spent most of her time inside with Grandma Bessie. Every so often, Luke would come in with an update on how the calf was doing. It seemed the poor little thing suddenly wouldn't eat and acted lethargic.

When it started to get dark outside, Grandpa came in, shaking his head sadly.

"The calf?" Leah asked, almost afraid of what the answer would be.

"No better," Grandpa Matthew replied with a sigh. He looked down at his boots and then back up at Leah, "Leah, I hate to ask this, but I can't get Luke to go home. Will ya try to talk to him? There's nothing he can do at this point."

Leah slowly nodded her head. Grabbing a lantern off of the table, she headed out to the barn, carrying a cup of water in her spare hand.

She found Luke in the calf's pen. He was sitting in the corner against the wall with the calf's head in his lap.

"Luke," she set down the lantern and handed him the water, "Don't you think it's time for you to go home?"

Luke shook his head slowly, "*Ach*, Leah, I've got to see if I can do anything else for Little Bit."

Leah smiled at the nickname he had made up for the little heifer.

"You have done so much for my grandfather...for all of us." Leah whispered as she leaned her arms against the calf's pen, "We can never thank you enough, Luke."

"It's been no problem at all." Luke assured her, never looking up to meet her eyes.

"What about work?" Leah asked bluntly as she watched Luke carefully stroke the calf's forehead, "Aren't you part of a construction crew? What has happened with that?"

Luke shrugged his shoulders and took a deep breath, "I told them I needed a few weeks off. They'll survive without me."

"Luke," Leah shook her head sadly, "Don't you need that money? Aren't you trying to save back for a place of your own? Buying your own farm won't be cheap; you need to take all the work that you can now while you're young and single."

"Nothing in life is promised, Leah," Luke finally said with a sigh, "I just want to spend each day doing what I feel like the Lord wants...and helping out your grandpa is something I feel like I'm supposed to do. That's more important than any farm of my own."

Something about the quiet barn and the mingled scent of calves and fresh hay left Leah feeling strangely like crying. And, watching Luke tenderly care for the sick calf, she realized that she might have somewhat misjudged him all along. Maybe his good qualities were a lot more important than simply having a beautiful body and a charming personality.

"It's getting late," Luke finally observed, "You should go on and get your rest. I'm sure you have a busy work day ahead of you."

"As if you don't," Leah muttered, thinking about Luke's upcoming schedule. Once Grandpa Matthew was awake, Luke would head back home and take care of his own family's farm before coming back to help more with the calves.

"I'll be fine," Luke assured her. Standing up, he gave her an awkward pat on the shoulder, "You just save all your worryin' for your grandparents."

Lying in bed that night, Leah couldn't sleep. Instead, she found herself constantly drawn to the window and the light she could still see burning brightly in the barn.

She tried to pick up one of her romance books to read about a couple who were madly in love, but somehow the words seemed hollow and empty.

Try as she might, Leah couldn't stop thinking about Luke.

Ach, Leah, what is wrong with you?, She asked herself as she worked to readjust her pillow.

She had made up her mind long ago that she was going to have a relationship unlike those around her. She was tired of seeing her parents living together as happy companions – Leah didn't want that for herself; instead, she wanted a relationship filled with excitement and passion.

Luke Schmidt would never give her what she wanted. Enos Yoder could.

But would it work?

BOOK TWO

Chapter Eight

Matthew made his way out to the barn. He was anxious to see if the little calf had made it through the night.

Opening the barn door, he stepped into the dimly lit area, waiting on his eyes to adjust to his surroundings. Walking over to the calf's pen, he discovered the calf standing up and drinking out of the bottle they had hooked in place on the side of the pen.

"Well, look at you," Matthew exclaimed, reaching out to pen the little animal on the top of the head, "I think you're going to make it."

Glancing into the corner of the pen, he noticed Luke sleeping with his back against the barn wall.

Ach, Luke had never gone home. Watching him sleep, Matthew shook his head and sighed.

"Luke," he spoke up, "Luke!"

Luke's eyes opened and he looked up at Matthew in surprise.

"Oh, good morning, Mr. Eicher," he said with a yawn, "It seems like I must have fallen asleep here in the barn."

"You're a pretty good vet," Matthew announced as he motioned toward the calf.

Luke smiled, "I can't take credit for that. I don't think anyone but the Lord himself can be thanked for that one. I was so shocked when she started perking up."

Pulling himself to his feet, Luke started to brush some of the hay off of his clothing, "I hate to leave before the morning feeding, but I have to get home and help my *daed* out with his farm work. I think I slept a lot later than I should have."

"You've done more than enough, Luke. Please, take the rest of the day off and spend some time at home."

Luke looked at him for a minute and then shrugged, "I may just do that. It would be nice to see my family for a bit."

As he watched Luke walk toward the barn door, Matthew found himself overtaken by emotion. There was something about seeing a young man so helpful and kind, so free of major mistakes, that Matthew couldn't hold back some words of advice.

"Luke," Matthew took a deep breath, "Always remember that you've got your whole life ahead of you...and one mistake can destroy your life forever. I know that better than anyone."

Luke turned around and walked back to Matthew's side, "*Ach*, Mr. Eicher, nobody goes totally without mistakes. I hope I can avoid them, but it's good to know that the Lord's always there for me no matter what. He's ready to forgive any of us...even you, Mr. Eicher, no matter what."

Matthew opened his mouth to protest, but instead he just gave Luke a friendly lap on the shoulder and said, "I'll see ya tomorrow?"

Luke nodded and was on his way.

Luke couldn't understand. No one could understand. Matthew knew there was no forgiveness for the way that he had treated Bessie. She had deserved so much better and now, with Bessie on her death bed, it was too late to ever make things right.

As glad as Matthew was to have Luke and Leah at his house, they had brought their own share of bad memories and feelings with them. Matthew had not been blind to the fact that Luke worshiped the ground Leah walked upon, or that his granddaughter treated Luke like she simply tolerated him. It broke Matthew's heart to see Leah treat Luke so badly. Certainly, he might not be the best looking or most outgoing boy in the world, but he held a certain kind of devotion and kindness that Matthew wasn't used to seeing in young men.

Matthew took a deep breath and shrugged his shoulders. There was no way he could change his past mistakes, and it seemed that there was no way to stop his granddaughter from making a share of her own.

Since Luke had decided to spend the morning with his family and Leah needed a bag of sugar to make a pie, she called a driver to pick her up and give her a ride into town.

Hurrying through the grocery store, she rushed to get what she needed so that she could get back to her grandparents' farm in time to make both a cherry and an apple pie before she went to her parents' house for the weekend.

She turned an aisle in the store and found herself face-to-face with none other than Enos Troyer. Thankfully, this time she didn't have Luke with her.

"Hello, Enos," she could hardly believe that she found the courage to say his name.

Enos gave a slight nod in her direction but continued on with his cart full of groceries.

Leah couldn't decide if she felt more like squealing with joy at having seen the wonderful-*gut* man or crying because he once again gave her no notice at all.

As she paid for her groceries, Leah felt like her fingers were made of rubber and she battled to keep them from trembling as she counted out change.

Toting her bags of sugar out of the store, she wondered if she should simply give up all dreams of ever having a future with Enos. It was beginning to feel hopeless, and her cheery mood suddenly turned sour.

"Hey, Leah, wait up!"

Leah turned around in time to see Enos walking her direction. He held no groceries in his hands, indicating that he had left them in the store so that he could pursue her. She had to pinch herself to make sure that she wasn't dreaming.

"Enos," she exclaimed, trying to hide her excitement, "did I forget something inside?"

"Leah," Enos took a deep breath and shrugged his shoulders, "Would you like me to drive you to the young peoples' gathering on Sunday night?"

His words were unexpected and, somehow, they almost seemed to hurt. Rather than being caring, it sounded like he was just tossing a suggestion out since she was his last option.

Leah took a deep breath, "Of course!"

"You're not going with that fat boy?"

Leah wasn't sure that she liked the way Enos talked about Luke, but she supposed that no one could be perfect all the time.

"I have no plans." She assured him, biting her tongue to keep from standing up for Luke.

"Someone told me he was your beau," Enos replied, running his hand through his hair.

Watching his every move, it was hard for Leah to keep her good sense about her. Enos was so much like one of the men from the romance books she read. She wished that she could flip forward the pages of her life and find herself held tightly in his arms, basking in the warmth of his embrace as he asked for her hand in marriage.

"So, you're not "Fatty's" girlfriend?" Enos' words interrupted Leah's thoughts.

Luke's girlfriend? Absolutely not!

"No," She was quick to say, "He's nothing to me. He just gives me a ride occasionally."

"All right then, I'll pick you up at your house around five on Sunday night."

Leah watched Enos go back into the store. She stood still until he had disappeared from view. Taking a deep breath, she fought the urge not to scream with excitement as she made her way back to her driver's car. She could hardly wait to share the good news with Amanda that very night!

As soon as she got out of the car and handed the driver the right amount of money, Leah took her groceries into her grandparents' house. Glancing toward the hitching post, she noticed that Luke's buggy was tied in place, indicating that had returned.

Despite the fact that telling Luke about Enos would not be easy, she knew that she had to cancel their plans to ride together to the young peoples' gathering. As soon as she had deposited her groceries on the kitchen table, she went back outside and started across the yard.

"Luke," Leah hurried out to the barn where Luke was busy putting down some fresh bedding for the growing calves, "We need to talk."

Luke stopped what he was doing and stood up straighter, "What's going on?"

"Well," Leah smiled to herself, trying to hold in her own excitement without seeming entirely rude, "I'm afraid we're going to have to do things a bit differently Sunday night."

"What do you mean?" Luke raised his eyebrows in confusion.

"*Ach*, Luke, I got invited to go with Enos Troyer. He wants to drive me there! I just wanted you to know so that you wouldn't come by to pick me up."

Luke stared at her in surprise.

"Leah," he finally started, "you and I have gone together every Sunday since you turned sixteen. I know two months may not be a lifetime, but it sure felt like something to me."

"Posh, Luke," she tried to brush off his words, "You were nice enough to give me a ride when no one else would, but now I have other options. You don't have to worry about me anymore."

Leah hoped that he would be satisfied with her answer and turned to leave, but Luke stopped her, "It never was a bother to me, Leah. You mean a lot to me. I thought maybe we were starting to mean something to each other. I thought maybe we had..."

Leah cut him short, "Luke, we had nothing together. You are a nice farmhand and you've helped me. I appreciate it, but there is nothing else to say. I want things you can't give me, Luke. I'm sorry, but I think it would be best that we simply not talk to each other anymore. I've already hired a driver to take me home tonight."

With that, Leah turned and left both the barn and Luke Schmidt.

Luke left early that afternoon. He didn't even come into the house to say goodbye before he left. Leah was glad for that. She spent all her time slaving over the stove, working to prepare a roast and finish baking her pies.

When she was sure that Luke was gone and that her driver would soon be on his way, she gathered her bags and went out to the barn to tell Grandpa Matthew goodbye for the weekend.

"Grandpa," She called out as she stepped into the barn and looked for her grandfather, "I'm almost ready to go."

"Back here, Leah," Grandpa Matthew called from the back of the barn where he kept the supplies. Somehow, his voice sounded different than usual; more strained and much less friendly.

Leah had a hard time deciding if she should check on him or simply leave him alone.

Making her way back through the rows of calf pens, Leah found her grandfather pouring some calf milk into a different container.

"I'm about to leave, Grandpa," she repeated, "I've left a couple pies on the counter and there's a roast almost finished in the oven."

"I heard what you told Luke," Grandpa Matthew announced abruptly as he scooped into a big feed bag with a metal dipper. Standing up straight, he turned to face Leah, "*Ach*, child, what do you think you're doing? You hurt that boy's feelings!"

His words hit Leah off-guard. Suddenly, she realized that he must have been in the barn when she confronted Luke.

Something about Grandpa Matthew's scolding got under Leah's skin and gnawed at her. She wanted to smart off good, but instead she managed to bite her tongue and simply said, "It's my life. I figure I have the right to choose who I want to go places with. Luke was only a friend."

"You didn't have to be so harsh to him, Leah. He's done a lot for this family."

Leah let out a huff, "He's done a lot for you, Grandpa, but I'm not going to devote my life to him simply because he helps you on the farm."

Grandpa shook his head, "Leah, you undervalue Luke. He's a good boy. You don't find many boys his age that would be so helpful and kind. He's thoughtful and he's probably one of the nicest men I know."

"I'm not looking for nice, Grandpa." Leah exclaimed, her temper starting to flare.

"Grandpa Matthew," Leah took a deep breath and plunged forward, "I know I'm being disrespectful, but I don't think you know anything about romance at all. I've watched you and Grandma Bessie my whole life, and I simply don't think you're one to be giving advice to anyone. As far as I can tell, you two have never gotten along good and you've never wanted to spend time around Grandma, even though she loves you. I want something better than that. I want sparks and romance and excitement! I want to feel like I'm in love...I don't want to feel like I'm just living with a friend!"

Grandpa's face got red and he stared at Leah in surprise. As soon as the words had exited her mouth, she regretted them. She looked down at her shoes in shame, dreading what might happen next.

Grandpa Matthew put his pitchfork aside and leaned his back against one of the wooden barn posts.

"You think I know nothing," Grandpa announced, "But I know a lot more than you realize. I know about the desire for romance and excitement...and I also know the cost. Just go on your way, Leah, your driver is here. You just wait and see if this is actually what you want."

Leah stared at him. She'd never heard her grandpa sound so upset before. His words seemed almost frightening.

She didn't even say goodbye; instead, she just turned and hurried out of the barn, anxious to get away from her grandfather. She wouldn't let anyone make her feel bad about her choice to spend time with Enos. She had looked forward to this day for months and she would not let anyone stand in her way.

Matthew took a deep breath and let it out, watching as his granddaughter climbed into the Englischer's car and pulled out of the graveled driveway.

He knew far too much about wanting romance and excitement, and it had cost him everything.

Celia. Matthew could still remember her name, although it had been forty years since he had seen her.

Matthew and Bessie had been married for only four years and already had two small children. Despite the fact that they had a very stable and committed marriage, the stress of farm work, babies, and keeping up with the bills had begun to suck the romance right out of their relationship. At twenty-four years old, Matthew felt almost ready to go insane as he fought through farm mortgages, disputes with the clients he worked for, and tried to come up with the money necessary to cover Bessie's stay at the hospital when baby Joe was born with complications.

Matthew had desperately needed an escape. And while Bessie turned to the Bible to give her comfort, Matthew had chosen an entirely different path.

Celia Jennings was the name of the college student whose parents hired Matthew to make repairs on their home that summer. Celia had long, curly dark hair and sky blue eyes. She spent the summer swimming in their underground pool, lounging around the house in her short pants, and chatting on the phone with friends.

Matthew had never expected her to look his direction. But one day she did.

Even now, forty years later, just the thought of what happened made Matthew sick to her stomach. He had turned his back on what was right. He had given up everything for the thrill of the unavailable. And now, Matthew was left with the empty misery of what he had done...and he could never be free of the burden.

Chapter Nine

Turning away Luke had been difficult and her talk with Grandpa Matthew had been almost as bad if not worse. The journey back to her parents' house left Leah battling a mixture of emotions. On one hand, she felt horrible to have broken things off with Luke. Looking into his face, she had been able to tell that his feelings were shattered. On the other hand, she was so excited about the weekend that she could hardly stand the wait.

Perhaps this was to be the turning point in her life. Maybe, after they had a chance to spend some time together, Enos would be prepared to start seeing each other on a regular basis. Maybe every Sunday he would pick her up at her house and take her home from the gathering once it was over.

Smiling, Leah could imagine sitting next to Enos with his arm around her, holding her close to his side.

By the time she turned eighteen, it would be almost time for Enos to propose. After two years of courting, they would make their love official. *Ach*, within three years, she might be the mom of a sweet little baby!

Leah could hardly hold in her excitement. She felt like she was floating on a cloud as she helped her mom serve supper and clean up the dishes. She could hardly wait to tell Amanda about her wonderful good luck; her little sister would be jealous!

"Have I got the best news ever?" Leah exclaimed as she crawled into bed, "Amanda, you'll never guess."

Amanda raised her eyebrows in the darkness and sat up, obviously anxious to hear the most recent occurrences in her sister's life.

"What has happened?"

"Enos Troyer asked me to ride to the singing with him on Sunday night!"

"What?" Amanda didn't sound quite as thrilled as Leah had hoped, "But what about Luke Schmidt?"

"Luke this, Luke that. *Ach*, Amanda, do you have to make things rough on me? Luke Schmidt isn't my husband and he isn't my beau."

Amanda was quiet for a minute before she stated, "It sure seemed like he was. Have you told him about Enos yet?"

"Of course," Leah snapped, suddenly wishing she hadn't let her little sister in on her big news. She had wanted to share her excitement with someone, but it seemed that she couldn't escape talking about the friend she'd turned away.

"How'd he take that?" Amanda asked softly.

"He didn't care." Leah lied, giving her pillow a good jerk as she tried to fluff it under her head, "Luke and I were nothing to each other, Amanda. He just spent time with me because he wanted to help me out."

"Hmmm..." Amanda took a deep breath and let it out slowly, "Well, then, I guess that's a *gut* thing. Congratulations on your date with Enos!"

Although Amanda was obviously trying to sound enthusiastic, she wasn't very convincing. Leah shut her eyes tightly, wishing that she could also shut off the thoughts that were churning in her mind.

Leah's mom had a bad headache Sunday morning so the family stayed home from church services. Although Mom had suggested that they go without her, Dad had been worried about her and suggested they just skip in case her migraine became worse.

Although Leah was disappointed that she didn't have the chance to see Enos, she was equally relieved that she wouldn't have to encounter Luke. Just the thought of him was enough to wipe away the excitement of the night ahead. Leah found herself hoping that Luke wouldn't com to the gathering at all, giving her a chance to enjoy her time with Enos guilt-free.

As the hours passed, Mom's headache became better and she assured Leah that she could go to the gathering. Leah breathed a sigh of relief at this news. If she had missed out on her chance to ride with good-looking Enos Troyer, she would never forgive herself.

When five o'clock rolled around, Leah was more full of jitters than if she was a jumping bean. Standing by the window, Leah waited anxiously for Enos' buggy to arrive.

"He's here, *Mamm*!" She exclaimed as the shiny buggy pulled in their lane.

"Have fun, dear," Mom called out when Leah pulled on her black bonnet and headed out on the porch.

"*Gut* evening, Enos!" Leah called out, her voice trembling with nerves as she reached his buggy.

Enos nodded his head, staring off into the distance.

Once Leah had settled into her seat, they started off toward the young peoples' gathering.

Leah kept fighting the urge to stare at Enos. He certainly was a handsome young man and she wanted to relish every minute of their first date together. She wished that Amish were allowed camera so that she could take a picture of this most precious moment to keep for the rest of her life.

Neither of them spoke for several minutes. Leah wondered if Enos was as nervous as she.

"It was mighty nice of you to offer me a ride tonight," Leah finally announced, feeling like some sort of conversation would probably be worth a try.

Enos gave a shrug and ran his hand through his blonde hair, "I had planned to take someone else, but she got sick. I figured you were better than no one at all."

Leah raised her eyebrows in surprise. The mood no longer seemed quite as special as before and Enos wasn't exactly sweeping her off her feet. Realizing that she was only being used because Enos had no better option wasn't the most romantic thing she'd ever heard.

Leah opened her mouth to say something, but Enos quickly interrupted, "I generally take some of the older girls, but I try to take everyone at least once."

The sky was beginning to darken as they followed the country road.

"I guess tonight was your lucky night." Enos announced with a half-hearted smirk.

Leah could not remember a time that she had felt less appreciated. Certainly, Luke was not the model date, but he had always made her feel wanted.

Suddenly, Leah started to wonder if she ever made Luke feel wanted. She knew that she hadn't Friday night. She had almost gone so far as to tell him that she wanted nothing more to do with him ever again.

Leah crossed her arm against her stomach, trying to breathe deeply against the sick feeling rising up in her throat. She tried to tell herself that it was nerves, but it felt a lot more like guilt.

When they arrived at the singing, Leah and Enos had said little more than a few words to each other. As they climbed out of the buggy and headed to the barn, Leah could not remember a time when she had felt worse.

Stepping to the brightly lighted barn, they were instantly welcomed by a group of young people playing corn hole. Several of the older boys came running to Enos' side, anxious to ask him to join in on their team.

Leah found herself looking around the barn, searching out Luke. Even though the idea of encountering him made her feel guilty, a friendly face would certainly be welcome.

"Where have you been, Enos?" Someone asked, "We were afraid you'd had an accident too!"

Enos rolled his eyes, "What do you mean?"

"Haven't ya heard the news?" One of the boys asked Enos, his voice full of excitement at a story to tell, "Luke Schmidt fell off the roof of his barn yesterday…that's why his family wasn't in church this morning."

"I bet that was a big splat!" Enos announced with a belly laugh, "I thought I felt the ground shake yesterday. I asked Dad if there was an earthquake, but I guess it was just old fatty."

Leah felt her heart drop into her stomach.

"Was he hurt?" She asked, no longer caring what anyone thought of her, "How is he?"

The other boy shook his head sadly, "They took him away in the ambulance, but he didn't make it."

"He didn't make it?!" Leah repeated, "What do you mean?"

"He died."

Even Enos became sober with that news.

Luke dead. Leah couldn't believe it. It felt like a horrible nightmare, and she found herself praying she would wake up.

"I don't want to be here anymore," Leah announced in a trembling voice, "I want to go home!"

"Forget me taking you," Enos replied, "The gathering hasn't even started yet. I'm not going to miss out."

"Fine," Leah turned and marched out of the barn. In the driveway, another Amish girl was being let out of a driver's car. Leah rushed to the waiting vehicle and asked for a ride home.

The entire trip, Leah could hardly bring herself to speak. The world seemed to be spinning out of control.

Luke dead? How could it be true? She could hardly stand the idea of life without Luke. He had become her closest companion, her work partner, and her best friend. *Ach*, over the summer she had grown to love him and now he was gone.

Love.

Leah closed her eyes against the tears that were flowing down her cheeks.

She had spent all her time dreaming of a passionate, romantic love like the novels she loved to read, and somehow along the way she had missed the real thing.

She thought about the last time that she had seen Luke and the way that she had treated him. Leah realized that she had treated Luke no better than Enos had treated her. For each time her heart had broken over Enos' rejection, she had turned and been just as horrible to Luke. He deserved so much better, and now she would never have a chance to ask for his forgiveness.

Driver Ben looked back in the rearview mirror and asked, "Did ya hear about the Schmidt boy falling off the barn? Fool thing was trying to fix some leak that was raining in on the lambs. Now, he is in the hospital and his family sure are mighty tore up!"

"In the hospital?" Leah interrupted his words, "Are you sure?"

Ben nodded his head, "Sure. I drove his parents there and stayed until just a little while ago. He's in pretty bad shape."

"But he's alive?"

"Oh sure! Good grief, Leah, you didn't think he's died, did you?" Ben laughed, "He's unconscious, but he's not dead. The doctors are running all kinds of tests and stuff. Now, you want to go straight home or stop along the way?"

Relief washed over Leah as she realized that Luke was not dead and, from what Ben was saying, might not even be in grave danger.

Leah was quiet for a minute as she considered her options.

"Take me to the hospital, please," she managed to speak up.

Ben looked back at her in surprise and shook his head slowly, "Now Leah, are you sure..." Before he could say anything else, he bit his tongue and just muttered, "I suppose you're old enough to make up your own mind."

Chapter Ten

Stepping into the hospital waiting room, Leah felt completely out of her element. Having never spent time in the hospital before, she was unsure what to do or where to go.

A young blonde-haired woman sitting behind a desk called out, "Can I help you?"

Glad to have someone she could turn to, Leah hurried to her side. She held her hands together, kneading them like her *mamm* would work the lump of dough before she started cooking bread.

"I'm here to ask about...to see about...I'm one of Luke Schmidt's friends." She finally found her voice, unsure of how to word anything.

The girl nodded her head sympathetically and gave a sad frown with her bright pink lips, "I'm sorry but unless I have the permission of his family, I can't give out any more details..."

Suddenly, a nearby door opened and Leah found herself face-to-face with Luke's mother.

Mrs. Schmidt's eyes were red and tears were streaming down her cheeks.

"*Ach*, Leah," she whispered as she reached out and put an arm around Leah's shoulders, "Dear, it is so good to see ya here. I didn't know if anyone had heard yet."

"I just found out," Leah whispered, "How is Luke?"

Mrs. Schmidt gave a shrug and shook her head, "He hasn't made any improvement yet. He had a pretty nasty fall and hit his head but good. He hasn't been conscious since. It's impossible to know when he'll wake up or what kind of damage the fall did to him."

Leah wondered how much Luke had told his mom about the way that she had broken things off with him. She was surprised that Mrs. Schmidt would even speak to her at all.

"Can I see him?" Leah whispered softly, "I need to tell him..." Her voice trailed off and she found herself battling the tears that threatened to overwhelm her.

"Of course you can see, him," Mrs. Schmidt returned, "Not many girls pay much attention to Luke. He's got a good heart, but he's certainly not what most girls want in a beau or even a friend. It did me good to see him have someone his own age to spend time with. He always spoke highly of you. No matter what happens to him, I'm just glad he had you as a friend."

Leah let Mrs. Schmidt lead her back into the emergency room and toward a small area with a number "5" written on the door.

"He's back here," Luke's mother whispered, "I'm going to go get some air. My husband is in the cafeteria getting us something to eat. We will be back soon."

Luke hadn't told his parents about the way that Leah had treated him. Obviously, he had left them to believe that she had remained a friend, leaving no room for hard feelings. Of course Luke hadn't told them. He wasn't one to try to gain sympathy for himself or get back at those who hurt him.

Leah took a deep breath as she pushed back the curtain and stepped into the small patient room.

Immediately, Leah was met by the sight of monitors, the beeping of different electrical devices, and hospital equipment. There in the midst of it all was Luke, his battered body lying on a metal bed.

Leah found herself wanting to turn and run the other direction. She had never been good in hospitals or around sickness. But, despite her initial reaction, she forced herself to go to the side of the hospital bed.

Luke's eyes were closed and his head was bandaged.

It was hard to imagine that, only days before, she had stood in front of him at the barn and let him know that she didn't care about him.

Pulling a chair to the side of his bed, she sat down and hid her face in her hands.

Ach, she didn't know if she could stand it any longer.

"Knock, knock," she heard a strange voice and looked up to see a nurse pop her head into room.

"Oh," the nurse quickly apologized with a smile, "I didn't realize anyone was here. I just wanted to check on him really quick. I'll be out in just a minute."

Walking to one of the monitors, she started writing something down on a chart.

"Are you a relative?" The nurse asked as she handed Leah a tissue.

Leah shook her head. She started to say that they were friends, but then stopped herself. After everything that had happened between them, she doubted he would consider her much of a friend.

"We used to go out together," she managed to whisper.

The nurse gave a sympathetic smile.

"Is there any hope he'll wake up soon?" Leah asked.

The nurse gave a shrug, "It's impossible to say at this point. We really haven't been able to gauge how much damage has been done or if he will ever return to normal."

The idea of Luke being like this forever was almost more than Leah could stand.

"Is there nothing I can do?" She asked, "Can he hear anything I say to him?"

The nurse cocked her head to one side in thought, "No, sweetie, I really doubt it...but it's impossible to be sure."

When the nurse left the room, Leah grabbed for a nearby tissue and started to wipe at the tears that rolled down her face.

"Luke," she took a deep breath, "I'm not sure if you can hear me or not...but I just wanted to say that I am so sorry. I am so, so sorry. I have been so stupid! You are the nicest, sweetest, kindest boy that I have ever known. I should have never treated you the way that I have. Everything I said in the barn was so wrong. I appreciate you now, Luke. I want the chance to spend more time with you. Please, don't leave me."

Leah held her breath, waiting for something to happen, but nothing did. Luke never moved or showed any signs of life, and she was left with only her tears and her regrets.

Matthew had struggled all day long. Somehow, seeing Leah destroy her relationship with Luke had made his burden feel even heavier than ever. He couldn't stop thinking about the wrong things that he had done. And, for the first time ever, he realized that he simply had to tell Bessie. She had to know that he was sorry for the way that he had treated her over their marriage; he to tell her that it wasn't her fault that things had gone bad.

Walking slowly into their bedroom, he watched his wife lying in her hospital bed. She had her Bible open on her lap, enjoying one of her better days. He wondered if his confession wasn't likely to make this worse. He wondered if hearing the truth might not completely kill his wife.

"Bessie," Matthew crossed the room and sat down on the edge of his bed, "Bessie, we need to talk."

Bessie moaned as she straightened up in her bed and turned to look her husband in the face.

"What's wrong?" She managed to ask, slowly closing her Bible and setting it to the side, "Is everything okay?"

Matthew closed his eyes and gritted his teeth, trying to gather his courage. Maybe it wasn't too late to back out...maybe it would be best to simply put this off or, better yet, avoid the entire conversation. Surely what he was about to say would only make Bessie feel worse.

"No, Bessie," he said slowly, "Things are not okay...and they haven't been for a very long time. Every day since you got sick, I have come in this room and looked at you and wished that I had the courage to tell you..." Matthew covered his face with his hands, "To tell you how very sorry I am."

Bessie was silent for a minute before she asked, "Sorry for what, Matthew?"

"Sorry," he replied huskily, "for the last forty years. I am so sorry that our marriage has been this way...I am so sorry that there were so many times when I wasn't there for you. I am so sorry that I never talked to you about anything. I am so sorry that I shut you out of my life and my heart. I am so sorry that I never gave you what you needed. I am so sorry that I wasn't the husband you deserved. I am so sorry..." the floodgates had opened and he seemed to be pouring out all his regrets in one breath, but he couldn't say anymore.

Bessie stared at him with a sad smile, "We had some good times, too, Matthew," she whispered, "Especially in the early years. The first five years, we had it really good. I think of those times often."

"But after that, things were awful." Matthew confessed, "And it is my fault entirely. And I am so sorry."

Standing up abruptly, Matthew wondered if he could simply be satisfied with that apology. He hoped that would be enough to sooth his guilty conscience.

Ach, Matthew, he felt a voice say in his heart, *you've come this far, go on and tell her the rest!*

Sitting back down, Matthew reached out and put his hand on top of Bessie's.

"Bessie," he whispered huskily, "I have to tell you the truth. I have to come clean about something."

What was he doing? What he was about to say might be enough to push her to her grave right away.

"There was a reason I grew cold," he confessed.

"What was that?" She asked, suddenly looking more alert than Matthew had seen her in many years. Any hopes he had of her drifting off to sleep were suddenly destroyed as he realized that she certainly wasn't ready to let him off the hook now.

"Bessie, I did the worst thing a husband could do." Matthew swallowed hard as he relived that awful summer in his mind once more, "I betrayed you, I betrayed our children, and I betrayed God himself."

Bessie raised her eyebrows, looking more like herself than she had since the cancer had taken over her body, "How so?"

Matthew covered his face with his hands, so humiliated and overwhelmed with guilt that he felt like falling to the floor in shame, "Do you remember the summer after Joe was born? I was working at a family's summer house down by the lake. They had this daughter who was home from college...*ach*, Bessie. You know how I had always longed for adventure and excitement. This girl was so exciting...so wild...and I couldn't help but look at her. What surprised me was when she looked back."

"What happened?" Bessie's voice sounded shaky. Matthew couldn't bear to look at her, but he knew that she was crying.

"I broke my vows to you, Bessie. Our flirting went too far and things happened that never should have. When summer ended, she went back to school and I never heard from her again...I promise. I am so sorry. I can't even begin to tell you how sorry I am. If you hate me forever, I won't blame you. I would do anything to go back in time and undo my mistake. I have destroyed our entire life together and it's too late for everything to be right again."

Matthew found himself overwhelmed with emotion. He covered his face, the tears soaking into his skin. Bessie didn't say a word. Matthew couldn't even start to image the emotions that she was experiencing; anger, disappointment, heartbreak, hate...it was impossible to know.

"Bessie, please, just say something," Matthew whispered, "Anything. I don't blame you if you hate me. I am so sorry. I can't even begin to tell you how sorry."

"Matthew," Her voice sounded soft and gentle. Certainly, it was obvious that she was crying, but she sounded much more composed than Matthew would have dreamed possible.

Looking up, Matthew saw something amazing in her brown eyes. Rather than hatred and condemnation, all he could find was softness. She looked at him the same way she had when they first got together, before his sin tore them apart.

Bessie reached out a wrinkled hand and took his in her own, "Oh, Matthew. I knew all along. I found out for certain right after she left."

She had known all along? Surely it wasn't true. But, looking at her worn face, Matthew knew that she was not telling him a lie. For the past forty years, he had not been alone with his sin – his dear little wife had known and had struggled through with him.

"Bessie, please forgive me," Matthew begged as he got down on his knees beside her hospital bed, "I can hardly stand myself anymore. Each day, I live weighed down by the guilt of what I did to us. I have destroyed our entire marriage with my mistake."

"Matthew," Bessie smiled as she stroked her finger back and forth against his weathered hand, "I forgave you long ago. I have just spent the last forty years, hoping and praying that you would tell me this yourself. I thought about confronting you, but I couldn't stand to do it. I wanted you to come to me. So many times, I hoped that you would truly understand the message of forgiveness and salvation. I have forgiven you, Matthew and, if you just ask, the Lord will be ready to forgive you, too."

The words were almost too much for Matthew to hear. He closed his eyes and leaned his forehead against his wife's bed.

Matthew began pouring out his heart in prayer, finally feeling enough confidence to ask God's forgiveness for the wrong that he had done.

Slowly, the guilt of the years began to melt away and Matthew's misery was replaced by the grace he experienced from both his wife and his Creator.

Chapter Eleven

"Leah," the voice of her father woke Leah from a horrible nightmare she was enduring. She opened her eyes to find herself in the hospital waiting room, "Come on, Leah, it's time to go home."

"Where am I?" She muttered, studying her strange surroundings.

Before her dad could answer, all the events of the day before came back to her. She had sat by Luke's side until the nurse had told her that she had to leave so that his family could see him. After that, she had retreated to the waiting room to stay until she was allowed back.

"I guess I feel asleep waiting," Leah mumbled with a shake of her head. Reaching up, she wiped another stray tear away from her eye, "How did you find me?"

Her father smiled sadly, "Luke's dad called to let me know that you were here. It's time to go home, Leah. It's getting very late."

"Luke..." Leah sat up a little straighter in her chair, hoping for the best.

"Still the same."

"I can't leave, Dad," she whispered, reaching up to cover her eyes as she was overcome by another round of sobs, "I can't leave while he's like this. I have to wait until he wakes up. I have to tell him that I'm sorry..."

"Grandpa Matthew told me what happened," Her father said gently, "But staying here isn't going to undo what you said. We don't know how long it will be until Luke wakes up. All we can do is pray, and that's something you can do at home just as well as you can here."

Leah didn't want to admit that her father was right, but he had a point. She couldn't just wait by Luke's bedside, ready to spring an apology on him the minute he opened his eyes.

She obediently stood up and followed her father to the swinging doors that led to the parking lot where a driver waited with a van to take them back home. Leah silently promised herself that she would pray for Luke like her life depended on it.

The next morning, Leah woke to the sun shining brightly in her window. Her head pounded from crying late into the night and her eyes were still sore from tears. Making her way down the stairs, she found her mom standing in the kitchen, working on a loaf of bread.

"*Gut* morning, Leah," her mom greeted, "You slept long enough."

Easing into one of the kitchen chairs, Leah took a shaky breath, "Any news about Luke?"

Her mom turned to look at her and shook her head, "No, dear. Nothing yet."

Leah leaned her forehead against her hand. Suddenly, the kitchen door opened, bringing Leah's face up. Her dad stood in the doorway, a happy smile on his face.

"Luke just woke up."

Leah let out a deep breath and breathed a prayer of thanks.

"Do you know how he's doing?" She managed to ask, "Is there any damage?"

"They're still doing tests," her dad told her as he sat down across from her at the table, "There's going to be no way to know for certain yet, but his dad says that he's talking and seems all right in his mind."

Suddenly, Leah felt awkward and shy. She realized that her parents were both studying her, waiting on her to say something else. She wondered if she should offer to go talk to him or if she should hold off until later.

"What should I do?" She whispered, suddenly realizing that the advice of her parents might not be the worst thing, "Mom and Dad, I have so much I need to say to him. I just want to get it over with!"

"I know you want it to be over," Her mother said gently as she eased down at the table beside Leah, "but I think it would be best if you just let Luke have some time to recover. You can talk to him later."

"He's not allowed visitors right now, anyway," Her dad added.

Leah nodded and rested her throbbing head against the palm of her hand. Her parents were right. The whole thing of putting someone else's needs first seemed strange to Leah. Her first instinct was to just get her apology over with so she could put her guilt behind her. Romance books certainly hadn't prepared her for situations like this.

The week seemed to pass by so slowly. Every day, Leah found herself thinking about Luke and wondering how he was doing. Although her dad talked to the Schmidt family fairly often, Leah always wondered what might happen between updates.

Since she had spent so much time at her grandparents' house, Leah's parents decided to give her a break and sent Amanda to help out for a while.

Surprisingly enough, it seemed that Grandma Bessie was making a sudden turn for the better. Leah had gone by to see her grandparents once during the week and instantly noticed a change not only in her grandmother's health but also in the entire mood within the house. Suddenly, it seemed that Grandma Bessie and Grandpa Matthew were close, enjoying time together and constantly talking.

Everyone was baffled by the change.

"I don't know what *Daed* did," Leah's father announced, "But it certainly seems that something happened. Mom acts like she might get better simply so he can make up the last forty years. Seems like they'll never run out of things to talk about!"

Thursday morning, Leah was busy helping her mom break green beans to can when her dad came in to say, "They brought Luke home yesterday. Mr. Schmidt says that he's about as good as new."

Leah let out a deep sigh. She had worried about him for so long that knowing he was well seemed almost too good to be true.

"He wants to see you, Leah," her dad announced, "Driver Ben's still out in the driveway. I'm planning to go see Luke's family...you wanna come along?"

Did she want to come along? Honestly, she didn't. Just thinking about everything that she had said to Luke the last time she saw him made Leah almost sick to her stomach.

Taking off her apron, she nodded her head, forcing herself to make the hard decision, "I'll be ready as soon as I wash up."

Their granddaughter Amanda was busy washing laundry when Matthew went in to check on his wife. Bessie was sitting up in bed with a book on her lap, but she was gazing out the window at the flowers dancing in the warm summer breeze.

"Have ya heard anything new about Luke?" She asked as her husband stepped into their bedroom.

Matthew nodded his head and gave a smile, "He's awake. Joe said that Leah's going out to see him this afternoon. Hopefully she can say what needs to be said."

"I'm glad you finally said what needed to be said," Bessie announced as she reached out and took her husband's hand in her own.

"I am too," he replied as he gave her hand a squeeze in return, "Now I have to go out to the barn and check on the calves."

Bessie pushed herself up on the pillow and asked, "Do you think I might be able to go out and see the calves?"

Matthew raised his eyebrows in surprise. His wife hadn't left the house in months.

"Are you sure you're up for it?"

Bessie smiled and nodded, "I seem to have gotten some new energy."

As soon as Bessie was dressed, Matthew led her out to the barn. They walked slowly, stopping often to take breaks.

"The world certainly is a beautiful place," she said with a gentle smile, obviously enjoying the sunshine.

"Matthew," she started, obviously uncertain about what she was going to say next, "I had just about given up on getting better, but now that I have you again, I realize that I really want to get well. I know that we don't have much money left, but would you be up for me going back to the doctor?"

The words sounded like music to Matthew's ears, "Bessie, if I have to sell everything I own, I will do it if there is even a chance that you'll get better."

Putting his arm around his wife, Matthew led her on to the barn so that she could see the calves. For the first time in forty years, he had hope.

Leah's stomach was in knots when Driver Ben arrived at the Schmidt house. It was hard to believe that, only a few weeks before, she had been there enjoying a delicious meal at their picnic table. Just being there brought tears to Leah's eyes. So many memories came rushing back; not just memories of that one day, but of all the days she had enjoyed time with Luke.

Mrs. Schmidt greeted them at the door with a broad smile on her round face.

"Come in, come in!" She exclaimed as Leah and her dad stepped into the house, "Luke's back here resting." Mrs. Schmidt led them back to the large family room where Luke was resting in a rocking chair, watching his brothers build a jig-saw puzzle on the floor.

"Luke, you've got company!" Mrs. Schmidt told him, bringing his attention away from his brothers.

When Luke's eyes met Leah's, she found herself feeling incredibly ashamed. What sort of friend had she been to him? Although she opened her mouth, it seemed that words would not come.

"It's good to see you again, Luke," Leah could hear her *daed* saying, obviously trying to fill the awkward silence, "Are you feeling okay?"

"Yes," Luke assured him, "I'm good as new. If I'd known how much my mom would spoil me, I would have fallen off that roof a lot sooner!"

They both laughed, but Leah could only stare at the floor and bite her lip.

"It's so good to see you back home and awake," her father continued, "We've all been very worried about you, and have kept you in our prayers. For a while, it looked like you might be staying at the hospital for good."

Luke smiled, "*Ach*, no! I stayed in that place long enough. If they hadn't agreed to release me yesterday, I would have just escaped when no one was looking."

Even though Luke's statement was truly funny and brought a round of giggles from his brothers, Leah couldn't even find the humor in it. She was so ashamed of herself – all she could do was stare at the floor.

"Leah," Luke cleared his throat, "Would you want to go outside to talk for a bit? Seems like a lifetime since I last saw you."

The last time he'd seen her, she'd been so awful. It seemed that she could hear every horrible word she had spoken replaying in her mind. She wasn't even sure why Luke would want to see her at all.

"Leah, what do you say?" He dad asked, giving her a nudge with his elbow.

Leah slowly nodded her head without looking up, "Sure. If you feel up to going outside."

"I feel up for anything," Luke's announcement brought a quick scolding from his mom.

"Watch him, Leah," Mrs. Schmidt exclaimed as they started toward the door, "If we don't keep a tight hold on him, he'll be out plowing a field!"

Leah and Luke stepped out on the front porch and Luke pointed toward the creek that ran beside their farm, "Want to go tadpole hunting?"

Leah had to give a half-smile, "I'll walk down there, but I think I'll keep clear of the tadpoles."

They walked through the tall, green grass together, side-by-side. When they reached the creek, they stood in silence, listening to the bubbling of the water.

Leah realized that she couldn't stay quiet forever. Taking a deep breath, she announced, "Luke, I am sorry about everything I said to you. I truly am."

Luke smiled and looked off into the distance, "My mom told me that you came to the hospital as soon as you heard I was there. You gave up your time with Enos Troyer to come see me."

Leah gave a shrug, "I didn't miss much to be honest. I think I might have been spending a bit too much time with my head in the clouds, because Enos isn't at all like I'd dreamed him to be...and, even if he was, going with him wouldn't have been worth it. I really don't want to spend time with anyone but you."

Although it felt awkward to say, once the words were out of her mouth, Leah breathed a sigh of relief.

Luke seemed to study her as he turned to look her in the face.

"Are you truly being serious?" He finally asked.

Leah nodded her head, a warm feeling crawling up her neck, "I won't blame you if you don't feel the same way about me anymore, though."

Luke gave a shrug as if he was unconcerned, but he couldn't hide the smile on his face, "You might have to wait a week or two for me to be up to giving you a ride in my buggy, but I guess we could hire a driver to take us to the gatherings."

"I'd like that." Leah agreed.

"Wanna walk out to the barn with me?" Luke asked, "I can show you where I fell. I never did get that leaky place fixed…might try climbing up there again."

They both laughed at his joke and Leah walked beside him as they made their way across the yard.

Epilogue

"Goodness, it sure takes you long enough to go get ready to see your own grandpa!" Luke teased as Leah sat down beside him on the buggy seat.

Leah grinned and gave him a playful slap. After more than a year together, she knew when he was joking with her.

"*Ach*, Luke," she mumbled, "It isn't every day you get to go to your grandpa's birthday party! I'm so glad that we're having a big get-together with all the family. I think it will do him good to see us all."

Luke nodded and clucked his tongue for the horse to get started down the lane.

"I've got some big news," Luke finally announced as they made their way toward Grandpa Matthew's house, "I finally put in a down payment on that farm we've been looking at."

Leah stared at him in surprise; she could hardly contain her excitement as she fought the urge to bounce on the seat like a little girl, "Are you pulling my leg?"

Luke shook his head, "Nope. I'm completely serious. It's still going to be several years until I can get it paid off and get started on a house, but at least things are headed in the right direction."

Luke went on talking about his plans for the future, but Leah found it hard to concentrate on his words. From the way Luke talked, it would be a long time until he was truly ready to get married and started on their life together, but Leah didn't mind the wait. So much had changed since her sixteenth birthday. Back then, she had felt like she knew so much and was so ready for love and adventure. Now, it seemed she was so much wiser. She realized that life as a married couple would take commitment, effort, and a whole lot of God's help.

Leah no longer wanted a man who created butterflies in her stomach. Now, she only wanted Luke Schmidt.

Reaching out, she took his hand in her own. Luke looked up at her, obviously surprised by the gesture while he was thinking of something else.

"Are you all right, Leah?" He asked quickly, stopping in the midst of a sentence about raising goats.

Leah nodded her head and leaned it against his shoulder, "*Ach*, yes, Luke. I'm just so terribly happy."

Matthew Eicher lifted a glass of water to his lips and took a big gulp. It wouldn't be long before his dear children started pulling into the driveway in their buggies for his birthday celebration.

Matthew had never been a big one for celebrations, but this year he was actually excited.

"Matthew, dear, what are you thinking about?" Bessie's voice interrupted his thoughts as she came to put an arm around his waist.

Despite her serious condition, Bessie had astonished the doctors and had made a remarkable turnaround. It seemed that Matthew's confession had given Bessie the strength to move forward and, when an experimental new treatment became available, she had been quick to agree to try it. For the first time in forty years, she and Matthew had been a team that prayed together, read their Bibles side-by-side, and shared their thoughts. When times had been tough, he had held her up emotionally. Now, Bessie was nearing one-year cancer free and had regained almost all of her strength.

"I was thinking about how excited I am to begin another year," Matthew announced with a smile as he turned to look at his dear wife, "Another year without the weight of my guilt holding me back. And another year to enjoy having you by my side."

Bessie smiled sweetly and gave him a gentle kiss on the check, "I love you Matthew Eicher."

"And I love you."

Together, they stood arm-in-arm, watching as Luke Schmidt pulled his buggy into their drive and helped their granddaughter down from her seat.

Yes, Matthew was simply excited about everything life had to offer.